46 789 025 9

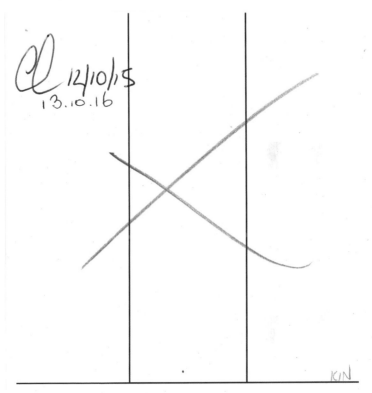

₡ 12/10/15
13.10.16

KiN

Please renew or return items by the date shown on your receipt

**www.hertsdirect.org/libraries**

Renewals and enquiries:  0300 123 4049

Textphone for hearing or  0300 123 4041
speech impaired users:

L32

D1420954

# THE HEIR
# OF THE CASTLE

# THE HEIR
# OF THE CASTLE

BY

SCARLET WILSON

First published in Great Britain 2014
by Mills & Boon, an imprint of Harlequin (UK) Limited,
Large Print edition 2014
Eton House, 18-24 Paradise Road,
Richmond, Surrey, TW9 1SR

ISBN: 978-0-263-24101-3

Harlequin (UK) Limited's policy is to use papers that are natural, renewable and recyclable products and made from wood grown in sustainable forests. The logging and manufacturing processes conform to the legal environmental regulations of the country of origin.

Printed and bound in Great Britain
by CPI Antony Rowe, Chippenham, Wiltshire

This book is dedicated to all those
little girls who ever dreamed of being Liesl and
dancing in the gazebo in a pink floaty dress.

# CHAPTER ONE

'THANK YOU FOR coming to the last will and testament reading of Angus McLean.'

The solicitor looked around the room at the various scattering of people, some locals, some not.

*Get on with it,* thought Callan. He'd only come because the ninety-seven-year-old had been like a father to him. Thoughtful, with a wicked sense of humour, and a real sense of community about him. He'd taught Callan far more than his father had ever taught him.

He wasn't here to inherit anything. He could have bought the castle four times over. He'd offered enough times. But Angus hadn't been interested. He'd had other plans for the estate. And after pretty much living there for part of his life Callan was curious as to what they were.

The solicitor started reading. 'Some of you are here by invitation. Others have still to be contacted. As you may well be aware Angus McLean had a considerable estate.'

He started with some charitable donations, then moved on to the staff that had served Angus over the years—all of them left sizable bequests that would see them into a comfortable age.

Then he cleared his throat and looked nervously around the room, his eyes deliberately skittering past Callan.

*Uh-oh. The castle. What has old crazy done now?*

'Most of Angus McLean's friends and relatives knew that Angus was a bachelor. It was always assumed—at least by those of us who knew Angus well—that Angus had no children.' He hesitated. 'But it seems that wasn't the case.'

'What?' Callan couldn't help it. He'd spent most of his life around Angus McLean. Never once in all those years had Angus ever mentioned any children.

Frank, the family solicitor, was clearly not designed for situations like this. His legalese seemed to leave him and he laughed nervously.

'It appears that in his day Angus McLean was a bit of a rogue. He had six children.'

Heads shot around the room, looking back and forth between each other aghast.

But a few heads stayed steady—as if they'd already heard the news.

Callan couldn't believe his ears. 'Six children? Who on earth told you that?' This had to be rubbish. Was a bunch of strangers trying to claim part of the McLean estate?

Frank looked him clearly in the eye. 'Angus told me,' he said quietly.

Callan froze. Every hair on his body standing on end. It couldn't be true. It just couldn't.

Frank cleared his throat nervously. 'As a result of Mr McLean's heirs—and with some further research—we've discovered there are twelve potential inheritors of the estate.'

Callan shook his head. No. Twelve people all wanting a part of Annick Castle. It would be sold without hesitation to the highest bidder. Everyone would want their share of the cash. Angus would have hated that.

'On Mr McLean's instructions, all twelve

potential inheritors are to be invited to attend a weekend at Annick Castle.' He bit his lip. 'With true Angus McLean style, they are to be asked to take part in a Murder Mystery Weekend—with the winner becoming the sole heir of Annick Castle. After confirmation of their claim with DNA testing, of course.' His eyes finally met Callan's. 'Mr McLean's last wish was that Annick Castle stayed in the family and was inherited by one person.'

The words chilled Callan to the bone. It was exactly the kind of thing Angus would have said—the only thing they'd ever argued about in this world. But Callan had always assumed there was no real family to inherit, at best, or worst, a few far-flung distant cousins. Nothing like this.

Chaos erupted all around him. Voices shouting and asking questions, people talking amongst themselves, pulling phones from their pockets and dialling numbers frantically.

There was a reporter in amongst the mix who walked out with his phone pressed against his ear. Who inherited Annick Castle was big news—particularly when it was being decided in such an unusual manner. It was one of the few privately owned castles in Scotland.

Callan stood up and walked outside into the rain and biting wind. His eyes landed on the building in front of him. Annick Castle. The place he'd called home for the last twenty-five years.

From the first night Angus had found him cowering in the bushes, hiding from the drunken, abusive bully that was his father, he'd welcomed him into his home. It had become his haven. His safe place. And in later years, when Angus had become frail and needed support, Callan had been the one to provide it.

Annick Castle was the place he'd laughed, cried and learned to be a man.

And it was all, doubtless, about to be destroyed by some stranger.

'Sign here, please.'

Laurie looked up at the electronic screen placed under her nose. She looked around; her secretary had vanished and the courier looked impatient. She lifted the electronic pen and scrawled her signature. 'Thanks.'

She stared at the envelope. It was hardly unusual. A letter from another firm of solicitors. She put it on the pile on her secretary's desk. It would need to be logged in the system.

She rubbed her forehead. Yet another tension headache—and it wasn't even nine a.m. She would be here for at least the next twelve hours. She sighed and picked up the court papers she would need for later and headed back to her office.

Five minutes later Alice appeared at her office door. 'Laurie, did you see who signed for this letter?'

Laurie looked up. It was the heavy cream envelope. 'Yip. It was me.'

Alice looked a little embarrassed. 'Sorry I missed it.' Her hand rested on her slightly protruding stomach. 'I've been at the bathroom three times already this morning.'

Laurie waved her hand. 'No worries.'

Alice smiled. 'I think you should look at this yourself. It's not work-related. It's personal.' She crossed the office and laid the now opened envelope on Laurie's desk. Receiving letters from other solicitors was an everyday thing. But none of them had ever been personal.

Laurie looked up at Alice's retreating back as she closed the door behind her.

Why had she closed the door? Alice had already seen the contents of the letter and unless Laurie was in a meeting with clients her door was always left open. It felt kind of ominous. Was someone suing her? But if they were, surely that would be work-related, not personal?

She picked up the envelope and turned it over in her hands. She didn't recognise the logo on the outside. *Ferguson and Dalglish.*

She pulled the letter from the inside. Heavyweight white bond paper. Exactly like the kind they used for legal documents. Her eyes scanned the page…'*as the daughter of Peter Jenkins you've been identified as a possible heir to the estate of Angus McLean…invited to attend Annick Castle…*' The next page gave contact details and a map of how to get there. The letter dropped from her hands. Her heart was thudding against her chest and she couldn't help but automatically shake her head. This was crazy. This was mad.

As the daughter of Peter Jenkins… Her father had died more than ten years ago. He'd never known who his own father was and had always been curious, but apparently his mother had never told him and refused to discuss the matter. Who on earth was Angus McLean? Was he the father he'd never known?

Because that was what this letter implied. What a way to find out.

She felt her stomach clench a little. Angus McLean could have been her grandfather. Why hadn't he contacted her when he was alive? Why wait until he was dead? It almost seemed pointless. And it was certainly pointless for her father.

Her fingers flew over her keyboard, pulling up a search engine and typing frantically. He wasn't hard to find. Angus McLean, died aged ninety-seven, one month ago. Never married. And apparently no children.

She let out a stream of words into the air. Really?

She scanned the letter again. How many children did this guy have? And had any of the others actually been acknowledged?

The phone rang and she ignored it. Whatever it was it would have to wait. She typed again.

A picture appeared before her and she took a sharp breath, her head moving closer to the screen. Annick Castle. On the west coast of Scotland.

Only, it didn't really look like a castle. More like a beautiful stately home perched on a cliff above the sea with gorgeous surrounding gardens and a swan pond. It was stunning, made of sand-coloured stone, with drum towers at either end and complete with cannons on the walls overlooking the sea.

She looked at the photo credit. The picture was taken twenty years before. Did Annick Castle still look like that?

Her curiosity was definitely piqued. What kind of a man stayed in a place like that? And why would he have family that he never made contact with?

She scanned the letter again. In her haste to read she'd missed the last paragraph.

*You are invited to attend Annick Castle to take part in a Murder Mystery Weekend along with eleven other identified family members in accordance with Angus McLean's Last Will and Testament. The winner of the Murder Mystery Weekend shall inherit Annick Castle, familial claim shall be verified by DNA testing.*

It didn't say that. It *couldn't* say that.

Lawyers all over the world would be throwing up their hands in horror.

She screwed up her eyes and pinched her nose, then looked from side to side. This was a joke. This was an elaborate hoax. Somewhere, in this room, there must be a hidden camera.

She stood up and walked around. First to the bookshelves on the wall, then to filing cabinets next to the door. She couldn't see anything. But weren't cameras so small now that they could be virtually invisible?

She opened her door and looked outside. Everyone was going about their business. No one was paying her the slightest bit of attention. It was a normal day at Bertram and Bain, one of the busiest solicitors' in London. Twenty partners with another thirty associates, specialising in employment law, partnership law and discrimination law. The phones started ringing around seven in the morning and continued until after nine at night.

Organised chaos.

The tiny hairs on her arms stood on end as if a chilling breeze had just fluttered over her skin. She closed the door and leaned against it.

What if this wasn't a joke? Eleven other family members. Who were they?

She was an only child, and as far as she'd been aware her father had been an only child too. After he'd died, her mum hadn't coped too well and was now living in the sun in Portugal with a little help from Laurie.

She walked back to the desk and ran her finger over the thick paper of the letter.

Family.

She'd felt totally lost since her dad had died. She didn't have a million relatives scattered around the world. There was just her, and her mum.

And now this.

What if she did have relatives she'd never met?

She tried to swallow the lump in her throat as she sagged back down into her chair. Dad would have been so intrigued to receive something like this. He'd always been curious about his father. It made her miss him all the more. She was going to find out the things he'd never known. Who was Angus McLean? Why did he live in a castle? And why on earth hadn't he made contact with his potential family members while he'd still been alive?

She was trying not to be angry. She really was.

She read the letter once more. Property law wasn't her forte, but could this even be legal? There were some differences between English and Scots law, but she wasn't sure if this was one of them.

A Murder Mystery Weekend to decide who inherited the castle?

There was no getting away from it: Angus McLean must have been stark raving mad.

She blinked. A bit like how she'd been feeling lately.

Maybe it was a family trait. The thought didn't really fill her with pleasure—only fear.

She watched as people marched past the glass in her office wall, all with a purpose, all with not a minute to spare.

Exactly as she felt.

How many holidays was she overdue now?

She straightened in her chair, the thick paper between her fingers.

Her father had been a grocer, her mother a shop assistant. No one had been more surprised than Laurie when she'd excelled at school. She liked learning. She liked finding out things. And she'd got swept along with the potential and expectations of her exam results. The careers advisor who'd pushed her towards university. The teachers who'd encouraged her to excel. Her father had cried the day she'd been accepted at Cambridge to study law.

And it had only taken her two months to realise that she hated it.

But, by then it was too late. She couldn't disappoint her dad. Not when he'd spent every waking hour working to help her achieve what he thought was her 'goal'. And especially not when she could hear the pride in his voice every time he told someone his daughter was going to be a lawyer. Turning her back on law would be like trampling on his grave.

She'd been miserable here for months. Always smiling, always agreeing to do more, to work late, to help others out. Never mind the hours she put in at the office, there was never really time off at home. Aches and muscle pains, sleepless nights, tension headaches, all signs that her body needed a break.

And maybe this was a sign.

No matter how ridiculous it sounded.

Her fingers tapped out the email quickly—before she had a chance to think straight and change her mind. She picked up the files on her desk and carried them outside.

Alice was worried. Laurie could tell by the frown on her forehead and the way her pencil was banging on the desk.

Laurie took a deep breath and gave her a smile, lifting a pile of Post-its from her desk. She started slapping them on the files. 'I'm taking some time off. Pink for Frances, green for Paul and yellow for Hugo. After I've been at court this afternoon there's nothing they can't handle. Ask them just to pick up where I left off.'

Alice nodded, her mouth gaping open as Laurie handed her the instructions from the letter. 'Can you book me a train ticket and sort out some accommodation for me?'

Alice put her pencil to good use and started scribbling. 'You're going to go? Really? When do you want to leave?'

'Tomorrow.'

'Tomorrow?' Several heads poked up at the surprise in Alice's voice from the pods around them.

Laurie nodded. 'I'm supposed to be there Friday through to Monday evening.'

Laurie Jenkins taking a holiday. It was unheard of.

Maybe it was time for change.


Callan stared at his watch for the twentieth time. This was his last pickup of the day.

Thank goodness. So far, there had been the loud Canadians, the over-excited Americans, the bad-tempered Irishman with the very sweet Irishwoman, and several others from around Scotland. Once the hoity-toity lawyer arrived from London he was all done.

He must have been mad. Why on earth was he agreeing to be part of this ridiculous debacle?

He sighed. What was the bet that Ms Lawyer was extra tired and extra crabbit? By his estimations she'd have travelled four and a half hours from London to Glasgow, another four hours from Glasgow to Fort William, and the last part of the journey on the steam locomotive.

He leaned back against the stone wall of the old station. He could see the steam in the distance. She could have stayed on the train from Glasgow—it did come on to Mallaig—but like any good tourist she must have preferred to take the *Harry Potter* train and cross the viaduct.

It wasn't really a problem. He couldn't blame her desire to see the stunning Scottish countryside. It just meant she was a later arrival than everyone else.

The train pulled into the station and the tourists piled out. Most of them would be staying overnight in Mallaig—a coach was parked outside the station to transport them to their accommodation.

It took a few moments for the steam and chattering crowds to completely clear.

Wow! That was Mary Jenkins? So, not what he was expecting.

Instead of an iron-faced middle-aged woman the smoke cleared around a long-haired brunette, with slim pink Capri pants, a white loose tunic and a simple holdall in one hand. Far from looking tired, she was fresh-faced and brimming with excitement.

Callan was used to beautiful women—he'd dated enough of them—but this was a shock to the system. Her clothes highlighted her curves, the swell of her breasts beneath the thin tunic and her Capri pants showing a hint of lightly tanned skin.

She walked over quickly. 'Callan McGregor? Thank you so much for meeting me.' She reached over and grasped his hand firmly between both of hers.

*Zing.* What was that? A wave of tiny electric shocks shot up his arm.

'It's a pleasure to meet you.' She waved her hands around. 'What an absolutely gorgeous setting. I've had an absolute ball on that train.' She pointed to the camera around her neck, nestled next to a gold locket. 'I must have taken around a hundred pictures.'

He was trying to remain calm. He was trying not to let the corners of his mouth turn upwards in surprise. It wasn't just that she was pretty—she was gorgeous. Warm brown eyes, clear skin, curls bouncing around her shoulders and full pink lips. 'Mary Jenkins?' he queried. The name just didn't suit her at all.

She let out a laugh. Nothing quiet and polite, but a deep, hearty laugh that came all the way up from her painted pink toes. 'What? No one has ever called me that! It's Laurie. Laurie Jenkins. My father called me after his elderly aunt Mary, but I've always been known by my middle name Laurie.'

He nodded. The Mary Jenkins he'd pictured in his head had looked nothing like the Laurie Jenkins standing on the platform before him. Around twenty years of nothing.

Was she really old enough to be a lawyer?

She shuffled some papers in the front pocket of her holdall. 'Let me take that for you,' he said as he reached down and swung it up onto his shoulder. It was light. It was surprisingly light. Maybe Laurie Jenkins wasn't planning on staying long? Unlike the Canadians, who appeared to have brought the entire contents of their house with them.

He ushered her along the platform towards his car, trying not to watch the swing of her hips and shape of her curved backside. *Focus.* That zing was still bothering him. Callan McGregor didn't do 'zings'.

He waited for the comment—there weren't many people with a pristine James Bond DB5 in this world. One of the few over-the-top purchases since he'd made his fortune. But she just happily climbed in the front seat and pulled on her seat belt. 'Do you know much about Angus McLean?'

He was thrown. He was totally thrown.

Not only had every other single person made a passing comment on the car, every other single person's first question had been about the castle—leaving him in no doubt why they were there. They could recognise money at a glance.

He should have walked away. After the reading of the will he should have left the solicitor's office and just kept on walking. Walked away from the madness of all this.

But something deep inside wouldn't let him. Whether it was a burning curiosity of what would happen next. Whether it was some bizarre desire to actually meet some of Angus McLean's relatives. Or whether it was some deep-rooted loyalty to the old guy, and some misplaced desire to try and maintain the integrity of the castle.

He waited until she was settled and then he pulled out of the car park.

'Well?' She was obviously determined to find out a little more. Her fingers were clenched tightly in her lap, her index fingers rotating around each other over and over. It was the first sign she wasn't quite as relaxed as she seemed.

'Angus was a good friend.'

She raised her eyebrows. The sixty-five-year

age difference was completely apparent and must be sparking questions in her brain.

'So, you're not one of his relatives?' She hesitated. 'I mean, you're not one of…my relatives?' Her voice tailed off and she shook her head with a little half-smile. 'I can't get used to the thought of any of this. It was only ever me, my mum and my dad. My dad died ten years ago. I never imagined anything like this would happen. It all seems so unreal—like I'm caught in a dream.'

'Oh, it's real all right,' he muttered under his breath. Then he shook his head and gave a woeful smile. This woman really didn't have a clue how he felt about any of this. 'I guess the *Harry Potter* train will do that to you.'

Her face broke into a wide, dreamy grin. 'It was fantastic. My secretary booked it for me. I haven't had a holiday in a while and she obviously knew I would like it.'

He tried not to let his ears prick straight up. She hadn't had a holiday in a while. What did that mean? Did she work for some hotshot company that made their employees work one hundred hours a week? Or did she just not have anyone to go home to? His eyes went automatically to her hand, but she'd moved it, jamming her left hand under her thigh and out of his sight.

'How did you meet?' Her voice cut through his thoughts. Boy, she was persistent. She still hadn't even mentioned the castle.

A shadow passed across his face and his lips tightened. 'I met Angus when I was a small boy. I spent quite a bit of time at Annick Castle.'

Something flickered across her face—doubtless another question—but something obviously told her to change tack and she let it go.

'So, what's going to happen this weekend? Are you organising things?' Did she think he was an employee? Even though he was offended, it was a reasonable assumption. After all, he had picked her up from the station.

He signalled and turned off the main road, passing some stone columns and an extravagant set of entry gates, and heading down a long, sweeping driveway.

He shook his head and his words were spoken through gritted teeth. 'The Murder Mystery

Weekend is nothing to do with me. It's being organised by some outside company.'

She shook her head. 'It's the most bizarre thing I've ever heard. Is it even legal? Inheritance law isn't my field of expertise, but I've never heard of anything like this in my life.'

'Neither have I.' The words almost fell out of his mouth. He wasn't embarrassed to say he'd spent the last week locked in a bitter war of words with Frank. But the solicitor had been unrepentant. He'd tried to talk Angus out of it. He'd talked him through all the legal implications, the challenges that might be brought against the decision. They'd even brought a doctor in to give a statement that Angus was of sound mind as he wrote the will.

But Angus McLean had been as determined as he always was in life. This was the way he wanted to do things, and nothing, and no one, could change his mind.

Callan could see Laurie looking around, taking in the impossibly long sweeping road to the castle, and the huge gardens. The car followed the bend in the road and she let out a little gasp, her hand going to her face.

'Oh. Wow.' Annick Castle was now clearly visible. Rebuilt in the seventeen-hundreds, the impressive building had over sixty rooms and a large drum tower at either side. It was clear the first glimpse of the castle took her breath away.

But instead of feeling secretly happy and proud, Callan could barely disguise his displeasure. Was she thinking that the castle might be hers after the weekend? The last guests from Canada had immediately asked what rooms were the best and whipped out a portfolio with extensive notes on the property. He'd almost ejected them from the car on the spot.

But Laurie wasn't quite so brazen. Or maybe she was just better at hiding it?

She shook her head, her eyes open in wonder. 'I just didn't expect it to be so big.' She pointed over at the sea wall. 'I knew it was supposed to be on a cliff top. I guess I just hadn't really re-alised how impressive it would be.' She fumbled in her bag and produced a tissue, dabbing at her eyes. 'My dad wouldn't have believed this. He would have thought he was in a dream.'

For the tiniest second Callan almost felt sorry for her. He knew that three of Angus's children had died: Laurie's father, another woman from England and a son who'd lived in Canada. Laurie was an only child, but the son in Canada had three sons and two daughters, and the woman in England had had three children. It took the total number of possible inheritors to twelve. All of whom were now here.

They pulled up outside the main entrance and Laurie jumped out automatically. 'I'll show you to your room and introduce you to the staff,' Callan said gruffly.

'My room?' She looked shocked, and then shook her head. 'Oh, no, I'm not staying here.' She started to fumble in her bag for her paperwork. 'My secretary will have booked me in somewhere.'

Callan was starting to run out of patience. 'She has—here.'

Laurie's chin practically bounced off the driveway. 'But I thought you'd just brought me here to show me where the castle was.'

He shook his head and shrugged his shoulders. 'It's part of the stipulation of the weekend.' Nothing he had any control over.

He waited until she'd extricated the crumpled paperwork from her bag and stared at it a few times as if she was still taking all of this in.

'Like I said, come and I'll introduce you to the staff.'

Her eyes widened. 'There's staff?'

He frowned. 'Of course there's staff. A place like this doesn't look after itself.'

That was the trouble with all these people. None of them knew or understood a thing about Annick Castle. None of them appreciated the people who'd spent their life working here. It didn't matter most of the staff had been left bequests, it was the actual castle that mattered to them—just as it mattered to Callan.

Laurie was still standing in amazement outside. The sun was starting to set over the horizon, leaving her bathed in a warm glow of pink, orange and lilac. With the beautiful sea in the background she could have been starring in a movie. With her dark eyes, long chestnut curls about her shoulders and her curves highlighted in her white tunic, Laurie Jenkins could prove quite a distraction.

She was the youngest relative here by far. And for a second he almost forgot that: the fact she was a relative—a potential inheritor. A complete stranger who would probably sell Annick Castle to the highest bidder as soon as she could.

It made the hackles rise at the back of his neck.

All day he'd picked people up and dropped them off. And there was no getting away from it. Some of them he already hated. They'd asked the value of the property, its potential price on the open market and how soon the inheritance would take to sort out.

So it didn't matter how Laurie looked, or how she acted.

The truth was—she was the same as all the rest.

What was wrong with this guy? Ever since he'd picked her up at the train station he'd acted as if she'd jabbed him with a hot poker.

She had no idea what his role was here. It was a shame, because if he could actually wipe the permanent frown off his face, he would be attractive. And not just a little attractive. The kind of guy you spotted at the other side of a room and made your heart beat faster kind of attractive.

When she'd spotted him at the station she'd almost turned around to look for the film camera. Were they shooting a new film, and he'd been brought in as the resident hunk?

She smiled to herself. His hands had been firm. Was the rest of him? It certainly looked that way—his shirt did nothing to hide the wide planes of his chest.

Mr Silent and Brooding was obviously not planning on telling her much. She was trying to push aside the fact he was impossibly tall, dark and handsome. And she was especially trying to push away the fact he'd fixed on her face with the most incredible pair of green eyes she'd ever seen. Ones that sent a little shiver down her spine.

But nothing he'd said had exactly been an answer, and now she'd finally met someone who knew Angus McLean her brain was just bursting with questions. It was her duty to her dad to find out as much as she possibly could. She followed him inside and tried to stifle the gasp in her throat.

It was the biggest entrance hall she'd ever seen, with a huge curved staircase running up either side around the oval-shaped room. These were the kind of stairs a little girl would dream of in her imaginary castle. Dream that she was walking down to meet her Prince Charming. If only.

Callan dropped his car keys into a wooden dish with a clatter.

Fat chance of that happening here.

She shook hands with a grey-haired woman with a forehead knotted in a permanent frown just like Callan's. Maybe they were related?

'This is Marion. She's the housekeeper. If you need anything you'll generally find her around the kitchen area.'

Laurie couldn't imagine a single occasion she'd want to seek out the fearful Marion but she nodded dutifully and followed him up the stairs.

There was an old full-length portrait at the top of the stairs of a young woman in a long red dress. Something about it seemed a little odd and she stopped mid-step. Callan gave her a few seconds, then finally smiled in amusement. It was the first time today he'd looked even remotely friendly.

'You're the first person that's noticed,' he said quietly.

'But that's just it. I know I've noticed something—' she shook her head '—but I don't know what it is.'

He pointed at the portrait's serious face. 'It's an optical illusion. *She's* an optical illusion.'

'But, what…how?' She was even more confused now.

Callum pointed to the stairs. 'It doesn't matter which side you walk up. It always seems as if she's looking at you.'

'Impossible!' She couldn't even make sense of the words.

He folded his arms across his chest and nodded to the other flight of stairs. His face had softened slightly. He was much more handsome without the permanent frown. 'Go on, then, I'll wait.'

She hesitated for a second but the temptation

was just too great. She could only pray he wasn't playing some kind of joke on her. She raced down one side and halfway up the other.

Her arm rested on the ornate banister, her eyes widening. The serene young woman was staring right at her—just as she'd been on the other staircase. She lifted up her hands in exasperation. 'But that's impossible. How old is that painting? Did optical illusions even exist back then?'

A cheeky grin flashed across his face. 'Did rainbows?'

She felt the colour flood into her cheeks and a flare of annoyance. Of course. Nature's greatest optical illusion. Now she felt like a prize idiot. Something tightened in her stomach.

She hated anyone thinking she was dumb. The only real joy in being a lawyer was the recognition that most people assumed you had to be smart to do the job in the first place.

But Callan didn't seem to notice her embarrassment. He was looking at the painting again. 'Angus liked to have fun. Once he discovered the painting he was determined to own it. It's nearly two hundred years old. He put it there as a talking point.' There was obvious affection in his voice and it irritated her even more.

Who was this guy? He'd already told her he'd spent some time living here. But why?

Why would Angus McLean take in a stranger, but ignore the six children that he had? It didn't make sense.

All of a sudden she was tired and hungry. The long hours of work and travelling had caught up with her and all she wanted to do was lie down— preferably in her bed in London, not in some strange castle in Scotland.

'Nice to know he had a sense of humour,' she muttered under her breath as she brushed past him.

'What's that supposed to mean?' snapped Callan.

She took a deep breath and turned to face him. 'It means I'm tired, Callan. I've been travelling for hours.' She lifted her hands in exasperation. 'And it also means I've just found out about a family that's apparently mine.' She cringed as some of the relatives walked past downstairs, talking at the tops of their voices about the value of the antiques.

She looked Callan square in the eye. If she weren't so tired she might have been unnerved. Up close, Callan's eyes were even more mesmerising than she'd first suspected and she could see the tiny lines around the corners. He was tired too.

She took a deep breath. 'I didn't know Angus McLean, but, just so you know, you might have him up on some sort of pedestal—but I don't. I'm not impressed by a man who lived in this—' she spun around '—and spent his life ignoring his six children.' She folded her arms across her chest. 'Nice to see he got his priorities in order.'

# CHAPTER TWO

JUST WHEN, FOR the tiniest second, he thought one of Angus's relatives might not be quite as bad as the rest, she came out with something like that.

Callan felt a chill course over his body as he swept past her and along the corridor. 'You're right. You didn't know Angus. And you have absolutely no right to comment.' His blood was boiling as he flung open the door to her room. 'Here's your room.' He stopped as she stepped through the doorway. Her head was facing his chest, only inches away from his. All it would take was one little step to close the distance between them.

It didn't matter to him how attractive she was. It didn't matter that he'd noticed her curves at the railway station, or the way she kept flicking back her long shiny brown curls. All that mattered to him was the fact she'd said something he didn't like about the old man that he loved.

But Laurie Jenkins was having none of it. She folded her arms across her chest again. 'That's just the thing, Callan. I *do* have a right to comment—because, apparently, I'm family.' She let the words hang in the air as she walked past him into the room.

Callan's blood was about to reach the point of eruption.

The very thing that knotted his stomach. Family. And the fact he wasn't.

He still hadn't got over the fact Angus McLean had six children he'd never once mentioned. The reality was he was still hoping it wasn't true— that someone would give him a nudge and he'd wake up from this nightmare.

Nothing about this seemed right. Angus had been the perennial bachelor, even in old age. Why on earth would he have children and never acknowledge them? It seemed bizarre.

Angus had had the biggest heart he'd ever known.

But then, he'd only known Angus for the last

twenty-five years. Maybe in his youth he'd been a completely different person?

It bothered him. It bothered him so much he hadn't slept the last few nights.

And now that he'd met some of the relatives it bothered him a whole lot more.

One of these money-grabbers was going to inherit Annick Castle. A place full of history and rich with antiques. A place full of memories that not a single one of them would care about.

Why hadn't Angus let him buy it? He'd known that Callan loved it every bit as much as he did. It just didn't make sense.

The family stuff. It enraged him more than he could ever have imagined.

Laurie was standing looking out of the window across the sea. Some of these bedrooms had the most spectacular views. He knew—his was just above.

And this complete stranger had just put him perfectly in his place.

She was right—she was family. The one thing he wasn't.

He dumped her bag on the bed. 'Dinner is at seven.'

He didn't even wait for a response. The sooner he got away from Ms Jenkins, the better.

Laurie breathed out slowly, releasing the tight feeling that had spread across her chest.

What on earth was wrong with her? And why had she just offloaded to the one person who could actually tell her something about her grandfather?

Common sense told her it wasn't wise to alienate Callan McGregor. He could probably tell her everything she could ever want to know—and a whole lot more besides.

She sagged down onto the bed. The bedroom was big, with panoramic views over the sea. How many people throughout the ages had stood at her window and looked out at this view? The sun had set rapidly leaving the sea looking dark, haunting and cold. Was it possible that the sea looked angry—just like Callan McGregor?

The history of this place intrigued her. It would

be fascinating. If only she could take the time to learn it.

Her hand smoothed the coverings on the bed, taking in the carpet, curtains and other soft furnishings. At one time these must have been brand new and the height of fashion. But that time had clearly passed. How did you update a castle? She didn't have a clue.

It wasn't that anything was shabby. It was just—tired. A little dated maybe. And obviously in need of some TLC.

Angus had been ninety-seven when he'd died. How often had he looked around the castle to see what needed replacing and updating? And how much would all that cost?

She shifted uncomfortably on the bed. She'd heard some of the conversation of the other relatives downstairs. They'd virtually had measuring tapes and calculators out, deciding how much everything was worth and where they could sell it.

It made her blood run cold.

This castle was their heritage. How could people immediately think like that?

She walked over to her bag and shook out her

clothes. She was only here for a few days and had travelled light. One dress for evenings, some clean underwear, another pair of Capri pants, some light T-shirts and another shirt. What else could she possibly need?

An envelope on the mantelpiece caught her attention. *Ms Mary Laurie Jenkins* was written in calligraphy. She opened it and slid the thick card invitation out from inside.

It was instructions for the Murder Mystery Weekend: where to report, who would be in charge and a list of rules for participation.

Under normal circumstances something like this would have made her stomach fizz with fun.

But how could she even think like that when there was so much more at stake?

The whole heritage of this castle was dependent on the winner. And the weight of the responsibility was pressing on her shoulders. She fingered the curtains next to her. She knew nothing about Annick Castle. She had no connection to this place. She wouldn't even know where to begin with renovations or upkeep. Or the responsibility of having staff to manage.

Working as a solicitor was a world away from all this. Everything and everyone wasn't entirely dependent on her. There was a whole range of other bodies to share the responsibility. Thank goodness. She couldn't stand it otherwise.

All of a sudden she wanted to pick up her bag and make a run for it. She shouldn't have come here. She shouldn't have agreed to be any part of this.

This whole thing made her uncomfortable. She looked at the invitation again. *Costumes supplied.* What did that mean? There was another little envelope with a character profile included, telling her who she was, and what her actions should be.

*1920s. Lucy Clark. Twenty-seven. Heiress to a fortune. Keen interest in pharmacy. In a relationship with Bartholomew Grant, but also seeing Philippe Deveraux on the side.*

It was a sad day when the pretend character you had to portray had a more exciting love life than you had.

It could be worse. Her card could have told her she was the killer. But maybe that came later?

Then again what did 'keen interest in pharmacy' mean? Was she going to poison someone?

Under normal circumstances this might be fun.

But these weren't normal circumstances, and now she was here, and had actually seen Annick Castle, the whole thing made her very uncomfortable.

She glanced at the clock. There was still time before dinner to freshen up and get organised.

Maybe once she'd eaten that horrible little gnawing sensation at the pit of her stomach would disappear?

Or maybe that would take swallowing her pride and apologising to Callan.

Maybe, just maybe.

Callan had finally calmed down. He'd had to. Marion, the housekeeper, had flipped when one of the ovens had packed in and she'd thought dinner wouldn't be ready on time. It had taken him five minutes to sort out the fuse and replace it.

Dinner would be served on time.

Served to the twelve strangers who were roaming all over the castle.

Which was why he was currently standing in his favourite haunt—the bottom left-hand corner of the maze in the front garden.

Callan could find his way through this maze with his eyes shut—and he had done since he was a boy. It was one part of the garden that was kept in pristine condition with the hedges neatly trimmed.

Other things had kind of fallen by the wayside recently. Bert, the old gardener, couldn't manage the upkeep of the gardens any more. The truth was he probably needed another four staff to do everything that was required. Twenty years ago there had been a staff of around six to look after the grounds alone, but gradually they'd all retired or left. And the recession had hit. And Bert had become very set in his ways—not wanting others to interfere with 'his' garden. In the meantime the maze, the front garden and the rose garden were almost in pristine condition. As for the rest...

He was thankful for the peace and quiet. All

of a sudden his safe haven seemed like a noisy hotel. Everyone seemed to talk at the tops of their voices, constantly asking questions. He'd tried to hide out in the library for a while, but even there he'd been disturbed by some of the relatives wondering if there were any valuable first editions.

If he'd had his way he would have locked some of the rooms to stop their prying eyes, not to mention their prying fingers. He'd caught one relative in his room earlier and had nearly blown a gasket.

A flash of red caught his eye, along with the sound of laughter and heels clipping on the concrete path. He took a few steps forward, crashing straight into Laurie as she rounded the corner of the maze.

'Oh, sorry.' She was out of breath and her eyes wide. 'Isn't this just fabulous?'

As much as he hated to admit it her enthusiasm was clearly genuine.

'How long has the maze been here? I had no idea something like this existed. It's amazing.'

He narrowed his gaze. He could barely focus on the question because his eyes and brain were immediately struck by the sight in front of him. The 1920s-style flapper dress skimmed her figure, hiding it beneath shimmering red glass beads. A feather was slightly askew on her head and he automatically reached up to straighten it. 'What on earth are you wearing?' Damn. There it was again—as soon as his hand touched the soft hair—the mysterious spark from earlier.

'This?' Her eyes widened again and she gave a little spin, sending a cascade of sparkling red lights scattering around them. She wrinkled her nose as she came to a halt. 'Well, I hardly brought it with me, did I? I got it from the costume room. Haven't you got into character yet?' She held out her black-satin-gloved hand to shake his hand. 'I'm Lucy Clark. Apparently an heiress and up to all things naughty with two different men.'

If he'd been anywhere else, at any other time, he would have acted on the current of electricity that was sizzling between them. He thought he might have imagined it, but his palm was tingling. He rubbed it fiercely against his thigh.

The Murder Mystery Weekend. The last thing on his mind right now. He hadn't even opened the envelope that had been sitting above the fireplace in his room. And he had no idea what room in the castle had been deemed the 'costume' room. His fingers burrowed into his jacket pocket and he pulled out the crumpled envelope. 'Oops.' He shrugged.

She shook her head. 'Come on, Callan, get into the spirit of things.' She reached out to grab his envelope, then pulled her hand back. 'I better not.' She leaned forward and whispered, 'I don't want to find out you're secretly a mass murderer.'

He shook his head and pulled the card from the envelope. He must have been out of his crazy mind to have agreed to be part of this.

Then again, he hadn't really agreed. Frank, the solicitor, had informed him that Angus had expected Callan to make his guests feel welcome and help oversee the weekend's activities. He'd had half a mind to walk away.

But his loyalty to Angus ran deep. Too deep.

If he walked away then he'd never find out who inherited the castle, or their plans for it. A tiny seed started to sprout in his brain.

Maybe being here wasn't so crazy after all.

Sure, inheriting a castle sounded good on paper, but once Angus's relatives realised the implications, the upkeep, the financial commitments, he was pretty sure they would all run screaming for the hills. Maybe he could make them an offer? He'd always been prepared to pay a fair price, and if Angus wouldn't accept it, maybe one of his children would?

His eyes fixed on Laurie. She was young. She was a lawyer in London. She wouldn't want to be landed with a castle in the Highlands.

For the first time this weekend he actually paused to think. Maybe he should play nice?

He squinted at the name on his card. He hadn't paid attention to any of the instructions about the Murder Mystery Weekend. 'It appears I'm Bartholomew Grant, thirty-three, a stock-market trader.'

A cheeky smile appeared on her face along with the tiniest flush of red. 'Hmm...Bartholomew Grant. Well, whaddya know? I believe you're one of my two adoring men.' She gave a little wave of her hand. 'Here's hoping you can play the part, Callan.'

The feather was bobbing in the wind. The shimmering red glass beads picking up the soft lights from the open doors of the drawing room. She hadn't donned a short bob wig in keeping with the time; instead she'd left her long brown curls snaking around her shoulders.

She was watching him through her dark lashes with her big brown eyes. His eyes dropped automatically to her left hand. He couldn't see anything through the satin gloves. No telltale lumps with giant diamonds. Surely a successful woman like Laurie must be attached?

She leaned forward again, this time the round neck of her dress gaping and giving a little glimpse of cleavage.

He blinked. What was he doing? Why was his brain even going there? He had far too much to think about this weekend. The last thing he needed was to get distracted by someone he'd never see again.

'Do you think you can play the part, Callan? Or is it all just too much for you?' Her voice was low and husky. She tilted her head to one side. 'Do you even know how to play nice?'

The words made him start. In another world Laurie Jenkins could be quite mesmerising. But he wasn't the kind of guy to fall for a coy smile and the flutter of some eyelashes.

'Maybe I just like to pick my play friends carefully,' he shot back.

She folded her arms across her chest. 'Well, that's a shame. You're the only person around here who looked as if they might be capable of holding a normal conversation. I couldn't get a word in edgeways with the Americans, the Canadians were too busy Googling antiques, and—' she flung her hands up '—the two people that I think are my aunt and uncle from other parts of England have spent the last hour dozing on one of the sofas in the drawing room.'

He couldn't help but smile. He'd already figured out she wanted to meet her family, but it seemed nothing was going to plan. He reached out his hand and grabbed hers, leading her over to a bench near the entrance to the maze and pulling her down next to him.

'What did you think was going to happen this weekend, Laurie?'

He could see her take a deep breath as she glanced around them. The splendour of the castle was behind them and even though the grounds weren't officially lit, the smooth front lawn, maze and rose garden were impressive to say the least. And she had no idea that just beyond that copse of trees lay a swan pond with slightly untrimmed foliage. She really had no idea about this place at all. She shrugged her shoulders, 'I thought this would be a chance to meet some family. There's only me and my mum now, and she lives in Portugal.' She gave a little shake of her head. 'She really couldn't cope when my dad died.' Her eyes had lowered and he resisted the temptation to reach over and squeeze her hand. But her fingers had already moved, automatically going to her throat and catching the gold locket around her neck.

He might not know her, but the pain on her face was real. She'd clearly adored her father.

She lifted her head, turned and stared up at the castle. 'I have no idea what my dad would have made of all this.' Her eyes were shimmering now with unshed tears. 'He so wanted to know about his father. His mum just wouldn't tell him anything.' She lifted her hand and held it out. 'This would have fascinated him, and the thought that he had other brothers and sisters scattered around the world...' She let out a sigh and shook her head. 'That would have blown his mind.'

Callan shifted uncomfortably on the seat. All of a sudden his reaction earlier seemed a bit snappy.

Now he understood a little of what she'd said. It seemed odd to him that Angus had never acknowledged the fact he had children. How must it seem to the newly acquired relatives? To know that Angus had provided for them in his will, but never acknowledged their existence?

He'd been so wound up with how he was feeling he hadn't given much thought to anyone else.

'I had no idea that Angus had children. He never mentioned it. Never mentioned it at all.' He pressed his lips together. 'It just doesn't seem like him at all. The Angus McLean I knew had the biggest heart in the world.'

'How did you know Angus? You seem a bit young to have been friends.' Her brow was furrowed, as if she was trying to sort out in her head where Callan fitted into all this.

He chose his words carefully. Her question wasn't unexpected. 'Angus helped me out when I was younger. And friends—that's exactly what we were. He was one of the best friends I had.'

'And you stay here—in the castle?' He could almost see the questions spinning around in her head.

'Not exactly. I live in Edinburgh most of the time. I have a house there. But I've always had a room here with Angus. He needed a bit more help in the last few years.'

There was so much more she clearly wanted to ask. He could almost sense her biting her tongue. Instead her eyes fixed on the maze and gardens in front of them.

'Do you know much about the estate?'

The words sent his hackles up. He tried not to let it show, but every question he'd more or less been asked by the relatives in the last twelve hours had revolved around money. He found it impossible not to grit his teeth. 'I know every field, every tree, every fence and every stream.

I've been in and around Annick Castle since I was a young boy.'

But Laurie hadn't noticed his tension; she was lost in a world of her own. 'Lucky you.' There was a wistful tone in her voice as she leaned back on the bench and looked up at the elegant façade of the castle. She sighed. 'This would have been my dream when I was a little girl, living in a place like this.' She held out her hand. 'I can only imagine what it must be like to play in a maze like this every day or to run up and down those fairy-princess stairs.' She gave him a mischievous smile. 'Go on, tell me. Did you ever slide down those banisters?'

He could feel his natural protective instincts kick in. Did he really want to tell her that he and Angus had regularly had competitions to see who was the fastest sliding down either side?

All of a sudden this was personal. These were his personal memories of his time here with Angus McLean. And he didn't want to share them.

He didn't want any of these people staying here.

He really just wanted them all to leave. The piece of paper in his hand crumpled under his grip.

She was puzzling him. She wasn't talking about money. She was talking about people and family. But maybe she was just cleverer than the rest? And what was more she was persistent. 'Or did Angus forbid you from doing things like that?'

The words jolted him. Jolted him from a whole host of memories that flooded his brain. Diving in the swan pond, trying to build a raft to sail across it, swinging from the rope swings that he'd made amongst the trees. Angus wasn't the kind to forbid him anything. He lifted his heavy eyelids and caught her staring at him with those big brown eyes. 'Only if he caught me,' he said quietly.

The moment passed just as quickly as it appeared. 'Shouldn't we be going?' He stood up. 'You've got a Murder Mystery to solve.'

'Oh, that.' She stood up, her dress catching the light again. 'I'd almost forgotten about that.'

How could she forget about that? It was the key to owning this castle. Surely it should be the first thing on her mind.

He led her towards the open doors to the drawing room. 'Let's get this over with.' She sighed, then turned around. Her hand reached up and rested on his chest. 'Callan, tomorrow, will you show me around the grounds of Annick Castle? I'm only here for the weekend and I'd like to see as much as I can.'

His immediate response caught in his throat, because his immediate response was to say no.

The last thing he wanted was to be the genial host, showing everyone around the castle he considered a home.

But Laurie seemed a little more measured than the rest. A little more interested in the history of the castle as a whole.

Her hand was still resting on his chest, almost burning a hole through the thin cotton of his shirt. She bit her lip. 'I was also wondering if I could see some pictures of Angus. See what he looked like.' Her eyes drifted off... 'I kind of wonder if my dad looked like him at all...' then came back to meet his '...or if I do.'

The hairs were standing up at the back of his

neck—and it wasn't the cool evening breeze. It was her. And the effect she was having on him.

Had anyone else asked to see pictures of Angus? He couldn't remember, but they must have—surely? If someone told him he'd a long-lost relative the first thing he'd want to do would be see what they looked like.

He gave a little nod. 'I know where some of the family pictures are kept. Leave it with me. I'll let you see them tomorrow.'

She gave a nervous kind of smile. 'Thank you, Callan. That will be nice. And the tour?'

Her big brown eyes were fixed right on him. She obviously wasn't going to let this go.

He wanted to say no. He really did. But how could he?

He could almost hear Angus's voice in his ear. *Show them around, make them fall in love with the place as much as we did.*

'Fine. I'll meet you just after breakfast.'

She gave a little nod of her head. 'Thanks.'

He gestured towards the dining room. 'You better go on. I'll be a few minutes getting changed.' He turned and walked off along the corridor.

Dinner with the twelve potential inheritors of Annick Castle.

He really couldn't think of anything he wanted to do less.

# CHAPTER THREE

BY THE TIME Laurie reached the dining room most of the other guests were already seated. It seemed there was no opportunity to pick your own seat. The calligraphy from the character envelopes had been carried on to the name cards on the table.

She gave a little sigh as she sat down. Her character was between both men she was apparently seeing, which meant that Callan would be next to her again.

A man around twenty years older than her sat down on her right at the *Philippe Deveraux* card. She tried not to smile. In real life he wasn't exactly her taste, but she held out her hand politely. 'Pleased to meet you.' She nodded at her card. 'I'm Lucy Clark, but I'm really Laurie from London. My father was one of Angus McLean's children.'

Her companion smiled. 'Then that makes you my niece. I'm Craig Fulton. From what I can gather, I think I am the youngest of Angus McLean's children.' He leaned forward conspiratorially. 'And I'm not sure that I'm comfortable with dating my niece.'

Laurie felt a wave of relief rush over her. Thank goodness. This could have been awkward.

'What do you do in London, Laurie?'

'I'm a lawyer.'

His eyebrows rose. 'Well, that will come in handy with all these shenanigans. Is this even legal?'

She shook her head. 'Scottish law and English law can differ. I'm just as in the dark as you are.'

The chair next to her was pulled out and Callan sat down beside her. He'd changed into a hunting-style jacket, obviously in keeping with the style of the evening.

But Craig persisted. 'But you must know something?'

He was making her uncomfortable. 'Actually, I don't. This isn't my area of expertise. I practise employment, partnership and discrimination law.'

Craig threw up his hands. 'What use is that to anyone?'

Now he'd really annoyed her. And it was clear that Callan was about to intervene, but she lifted her hand and laid it on his jacket sleeve to stop him. She smiled sweetly at Craig and spoke quietly. 'Why don't you ask my last client? I won him an award of half a million pounds.'

Craig choked on the wine he was currently necking down at a rate of knots. Leaving his neighbour on the other side sharply hitting his back for him.

Callan shot her a smile. 'Touché,' he whispered.

She smiled. 'I'm nobody's shrinking violet...' she leaned forward to whisper in his ear '...and I hate anyone implying otherwise.'

Callan lifted his glass. 'I'll remember that.'

The food appeared moments later, all served by a harassed-looking Marion and a young girl who looked too terrified to speak.

Everything was beautiful. From the chicken liver pâté, to the chicken breast stuffed with haggis. All accompanied by copious amounts of free-flowing wine.

After such a long journey Laurie could feel the wine go straight to her head and stopped after the second glass.

The doors to the garden had been left wide open, and, instead of feeling cold, Laurie found herself appreciating the clean sea air that circulated around them. It was the first time in for ever she could remember having a clear head. Sure, if she'd drunk much more wine it could have made her wobbly, but for the first time in months she didn't feel at her muggiest, with a persistent headache thumping in the background.

She tried to remember when the headache had actually left her. It had been there so frequently she couldn't recall. She really should get out of the city more. Was it on the steam railway that she'd finally felt her head clear? Maybe there was a lot to be said about highland views and sea breezes.

It didn't matter that the air in the room was fraught with tension. It didn't matter that she was lost amongst a sea of relatives, some of whom she wasn't sure she even liked. It didn't even matter to her that Callan was constantly prickly around her.

This was the first time, in a long time, she finally felt relaxed. Her body almost didn't recognise the signs. What she really wanted to do right now was climb the curved staircase, open her bedroom window to the sea air and slip under the covers of that comfortable-looking double bed.

She almost didn't care about the inheritance aspect of the journey.

Almost.

Because from the moment she'd set foot in this place she'd loved it.

It made her toes tingle. It made her breath catch in her throat. It made the tiny little hairs on her arms stand on end.

She couldn't even begin to imagine the fabulous history of a place like this. And all she wanted to do was drink it in.

And if that meant having to play nice with Mr Callan McGregor, then she would. Because he seemed to be the only person who could tell her what she wanted to know.

The dinner passed by in a flash, then Frank the solicitor appeared again and ushered them all into the drawing room.

Laurie almost let out a sigh. It was after nine o'clock at night and after a long day's travel she really just wanted to go to sleep.

She'd tried to speak to Frank earlier but it had been very apparent he didn't want to be seen in discussion with her. Maybe he was worried he would get accused of showing her favour because she was a fellow professional? All she'd wanted to ask him was a little about Angus McLean. But it wasn't to be.

Frank read out a list of rules about the Murder Mystery Weekend, about them staying in character and when they would be expected to meet. He also introduced some people from the company running the weekend's activities: Ashley, a blonde woman in a pale pink 1920s dress, Robin, a dark-haired man dressed in hunting regalia and John, who was dressed as a butler.

Tea and coffee were provided on a table at the side and Laurie made her way over to grab a cup. The rest of the guests were told to mingle and familiarise themselves with each other. As she poured the coffee into one of the pale blue china cups another one was slid alongside.

'Pour me one too, would you? I'm going to fall asleep in here. Playing nice doesn't agree with me.'

Laurie smiled at Callan's voice. 'You and me both. I had no idea I'd be so tired after the journey. All I want to do right now is go to bed.'

Should she have said that out loud? There was kind of an amused glint in Callan's eyes. For a second she felt a flare of panic. What did he think she meant? For a horrible moment she thought he might have taken it as an invitation. The colour started to flood into her cheeks, and she did what she always did when she was embarrassed—she babbled.

'It's such a long journey up by train. The steam locomotive was fabulous, I wouldn't have missed the gorgeous scenery for anything, but when it gets to this time at night, and especially after that beautiful dinner, I just want to go and lie down. Alone—I mean,' she added hastily.

But Callan was laughing and shaking his head. It was obvious he'd picked up on her anxiety.

She said the first thing that came into her head. 'What about you, Callan? Is there a Mrs McGregor to go home to?'

Had she actually just said that out loud? Please let the ground open up and swallow her whole. Wine and tiredness obviously weren't a good mix for her.

Callan shook his head, and was it her imagination or did he just glance at her left hand?

'No. There's no Mrs McGregor. I've been a bit of a workaholic these last few years.'

'And any mini McGregors?' In for a penny, in for a pound. It seemed prudent to ask, particularly after what had been learned about Angus McLean in the last few weeks.

There was no hesitation. He shook his head. 'I can assure you, if I had any kids they would be permanently attached to my hip.'

There was no mistaking that answer. Callan McGregor would never do what Angus McLean had—whatever his reasons might have been.

'What about you, Laurie? Are you like your

character—do you have more than one attach-ment?' There was a cheeky glint in his eyes as he asked the question.

Laurie rolled her eyes. 'I should be so lucky. I don't have enough hours in the day for myself let alone anyone else. Do you know, I think this is the first time I haven't had a headache in months.'

He leaned forward. 'It's all this good Scots air. It does wonders for your health.' For a second, her breath was caught in her throat as the aroma of his woody aftershave invaded her senses. It was delicious.

She gathered herself and smiled. 'Yeah, but it's making me exceedingly tired.'

'You mean you don't want to go and play nice with the relatives?'

Laurie took a deep breath. She knew the cor-rect answer to this question, but it just couldn't form on her lips. She gave a little shrug. 'Yes, yes, I do. But right now I'm just too tired to care.' She looked over to the middle of the room where they were all currently holding court, talking—no, shouting—at the tops of their voices.

She gestured over to the other side of the room.

'The person I'd really like to sit down with at some point is Mary from Ireland. She'll have been my father's half-sister. And she looks really like him. I'd like to get a chance to talk properly to her.'

The lights flickered out and the room was plunged into darkness, followed by a theatrical scream. And even though she should have half expected it, it really did make her jump.

Callan's arm slid around her waist. Even though she couldn't see a thing, she could sense him leaning closer to her. And it was her natural instinct to move a little closer to him. 'You okay, Laurie?' His warm breath tickled her cheek. More of the aftershave. It was scrambling her senses and rapidly turning into her new favourite smell.

She clutched the cup in her hands. Her hands had started to tremble. The last thing she wanted to do was shatter some priceless china on the parquet flooring. 'Yes, thanks,' she whispered.

'I'm sure this will all be over in a second...' his voice was low, the curls around her ear vibrating with his tone '...and hopefully then we can all get off to bed.'

The words sent a shiver down her spine. Something she hadn't felt in a long time. Something she hadn't had *time* to feel in a long time.

The realisation was startling.

She'd only been here one evening and everything about this place was surprising her.

She'd yet to feel a connection to any of her relatives—the one thing she would actually have liked.

But she couldn't get over the connection and tingle she'd felt to this place from the moment she'd stepped inside. She was under no illusion that Annick Castle would actually ever be hers. But she hadn't expected the place to take her breath away. She hadn't expected to get the tiniest sensation of belonging from just looking out of a window across an ocean.

None of that made any sense.

But what made even less sense was the man standing next to her, and the fact her skin was on fire beneath his fingertips. She didn't even know him. She wasn't sure if she even *liked* him. He was grumpy. He was prickly.

But something made her feel as if Callan

McGregor was the one true person about here she could trust.

Then there was the fact she knew he was single. It seemed to have made her stomach do dangerous somersaults.

And he seemed fiercely loyal to a man she knew nothing about.

The lights flickered back on around them. It only took her eyes a few seconds to adjust. The blonde woman Ashley from earlier was now lying on the floor, with a blood stain on her dress. Thank goodness she could still see the woman's slight chest rising and falling, otherwise she might have been totally convinced.

Robin—the man in hunting clothes—immediately launched into his act. 'Call the police, there's been a murder! Everyone stay where you are—you'll all be questioned.'

Callan took a deep breath. 'Oh, joy. Let the mayhem begin.' He was shaking his head again and he moved his arm from her waist. She was surprised by how much she could feel the imprint of his hand on her side. She was even more surprised by how much she still wanted it to be there.

He took a few steps over to the door, looking back across the room. There was something in his eyes, and she couldn't tell what. Was it a memory? Happiness or sadness? No, it was something else, a wistfulness.

'Angus would have loved this,' he said under his breath as he headed out of the door.

# CHAPTER FOUR

LAURIE PUSHED OPEN the door to the kitchen. It was ridiculously early but there seemed to be a whole army of pigeons nestling outside her castle window. And the truth was she'd had the best night's sleep in a long time. Whether it was the good Scottish clean air, or the immensely comfortably mattress, something had made her feel as if she were sleeping in a luxury hotel.

Marion the housekeeper was *not* in a sunny mood. She glanced at her watch. 'It's only six. Do you want breakfast already?' Her face was red, her brow wrinkled and her shoulders hunched as if an elephant were sitting on top of them. And there was a tiny little red vein throbbing at the side of her eye. The woman looked as if she were about to spontaneously combust.

Laurie crossed the huge kitchen and laid her hand on Marion's arm. 'No, of course not, Marion. I'm more than capable of fixing my own breakfast.'

Totally the wrong thing to say.

'That's what I'm here for, that's what I get paid for! You shouldn't be in here at all.' Her feet were crossing the kitchen in shuffling steps like a tiny little wind-up toy. 'I've got sixteen people to fix breakfast for and four staff. Then there's the morning coffee and cakes and all the veg to prepare for lunch. The butcher meat hasn't arrived yet and someone pushed *this* under the kitchen door.' She brandished a crumpled piece of paper in her hands. 'I mean, how many allergies can one person have? What on earth am I supposed to do? And did they have these allergies last night? Because no one said a word then—and all the plates came back clean. How am I supposed to deal with that?'

Laurie nodded her head and took the piece of paper from Marion's hand. She blinked at the list. It was the kind of thing that got printed in national newspapers when movie stars handed them to their chefs. She glanced at the name and stifled her smile.

She put the piece of paper on the table and tried to smooth it with her hand. 'Why don't you let me deal with this, Marion?' She met the woman's angry eyes. 'Let's face it, if they were this allergic to food they probably died in their bed last night after the amount they put away at dinner.'

There it was. The tiniest glimmer of a smile. The slightest sag of her shoulders showing a bit of relief. 'Do you think?'

Laurie nodded. 'Leave it with me. If there's anything that is a true allergy and not just a preference or a request, I'll let you know.'

She looked around the kitchen, trying to choose her words carefully. 'Is there anyone else to give you a hand? You're not expecting to do all this yourself?'

Marion bristled and Laurie winced, bracing herself for another onslaught. But it didn't come. It was almost as if it hovered in the air for a few seconds before Marion took a deep breath and calmed herself down.

'One of the girls from the village nearby is coming to help out. She should be here at seven.

She's good with breakfasts—just not so good with baking.'

Laurie ran her hand along one of the dark wood worktops leading to the Belfast sinks. There was a huge Aga stove taking up one end of the kitchen and a gas hob with sixteen burners in the island in the middle. There was a huge range of copper-bottomed pans hanging along one wall and shining silver utensils hanging along another. At some point this kitchen had been renovated, keeping the best of the old with the most practical of the new. It was the kind of kitchen used in TV shows, or period dramas.

She loved it. She absolutely loved it.

There was a navy and white striped apron hanging on a hook at the side and she picked it up and put it over her head. 'Okay, if you have help with the breakfasts that should be fine. I'm happy to help with the baking. What kind of thing would you like?' She bent down and started opening cupboards looking for cake tins and mixing bowls. 'I can do carrot cake, fruit loafs, lemon drizzle, cupcakes, tray bakes or sponges.'

She straightened up. Marion was looking at

her in horror. 'You can't possibly help with the baking. You're a guest.' She looked as if she was about to keel over and faint.

Laurie smiled and shook her head. 'And you're a member of staff that has had their workload increase tenfold overnight.' She sighed. 'Let me help you, Marion. Baking is about the only skill I have to offer.' She shrugged. 'To be honest I'm not that enamoured by some of my potential relatives and I'd prefer to stay out of the way in the meantime.' She glanced out of the kitchen window and across to the beautiful rose gardens. 'I'd much prefer to be in here.'

Marion frowned. The wrinkles in her forehead like deeply dug troughs. It seemed to be the natural position her face returned to after every interaction. 'You really want to help?'

Laurie nodded. 'I really want to help.' Just being in the kitchen helped. She could already feel some of the tension starting to leave her body, particularly around her neck and shoulders. The thought of staying in the kitchen and not having to participate in small talk with the crazy relatives was like a weight off her back.

The thought of not being under the watchful glare of Callan McGregor was also playing around the back of her mind. Why did he bother her? Why was he floating around in her thoughts? And more importantly, why had he hovered around the edges of her dreams last night?

Marion thudded a stained and battered recipe book onto the worktop. 'Can you follow a recipe?'

Laurie smiled. 'Of course I can.'

And that was it.

Acceptance. Acceptance into the murky depths of the castle kitchens.

Marion bustled around her. 'You'll find all your ingredients in here...' she opened the door to a huge walk-in pantry '...all your fresh goods in here...' another door to a chilled walk-in larder '...and all the equipment you'll need here.' She flung open a door to every baker's dream—a full array of scales, mixing bowls and every baking implement known to man.

Marion folded her arms. 'We've just had a delivery of strawberries. How do you feel about making a fresh cream and strawberry sponge?'

'Sounds good.' Her mouth was watering already.

'And an iced gingerbread and some flapjacks too?' The frown was on its way back.

Laurie nodded. 'No problem, Marion. Leave it with me.'

Marion gave her a little nod and bustled off to the other side of the kitchen where the girl from the village had arrived and was hanging up her coat.

Laurie started to gather all the things she would need. Peace perfect peace. Just what she wanted.

Callan pushed open the door to the kitchen and immediately started to choke, the thick white smoke clawing and catching at the back of his throat.

But it wasn't smoke, and the immediate burst of pure adrenaline started to fade. In amongst the white cloud around him, all he could hear was raucous laughter.

And what was more he recognised that laughter. He just hadn't heard it in a while.

Marion's laugh seemed to come from the very bottom of her feet and reach all the way up her tiny frame to the top of her head. It was a deep, hearty laugh that should come from someone double her size. And he loved it.

Callan waved his hands in front of his face, trying to clear the white, smoky haze.

'Marion? Are you all right in there?'

There was another sound, another laugh. This one verging on hysteria. And he recognised it too. He'd heard it at the train station yesterday.

The white haze gradually cleared, settling around his shoulders and every surface in the kitchen in a fine white powder.

Marion was holding onto the side of one of the worktops to keep herself from falling over. Laurie was sitting in the middle of the floor, a huge sack of white flour burst all around her, covering her hair, face, shoulders and legs and making her look like a snowman in the middle of summer.

He shook his head, taking in the scene around him. 'What on earth happened?'

Laurie opened her mouth to speak, then burst into a fit of laughter again.

Marion shook her head. 'Miss High-and-Mighty on the floor didn't realise quite how heavy the flour sacks were. She thought she could just pick it up and throw it over her shoulder.' Her shoulders started to shake again. Even though she was dusted in white powder her cheeks were flushed with colour. She rolled her eyes. 'Seems like the sack taught her a lesson.' She started laughing again.

Callan held out his hand. 'Laurie? Are you okay?'

Her slim hand fitted easily inside his and he gave her a firm tug to pull her up from the floor.

'Whoop!'

Maybe the tug was a little more than he realised, as she catapulted straight towards him, her flour-coated hands landing squarely in the middle of his navy jumper. 'Oops, sorry, Callan.'

She even had flour smudged on her nose. And he resisted the temptation to wipe it clean.

'What are you doing in the kitchen, Laurie?'

She tried to shake off some of the flour. 'I'm

helping. I got up early and offered to help Marion with the baking for later.'

'You did?' He was astounded. It was the last thing he was expecting.

Laurie was a potential inheritor of the castle and estate. Why on earth would she want to be helping in the kitchen? She was a lawyer, for goodness' sake. His suspicions were immediately aroused.

She reached over and started trying to brush the flour from the front of his jumper. Long sweeps with the palm of her hand across the breadth of his chest, sweeping lower and lower... His body gave a jolt at his immediate reaction. He stepped back. Seemed as if it wasn't only his suspicions that could be aroused around Laurie Jenkins.

He lifted his hands and brushed the cloud of flour off for himself. 'Leave it,' he said a little more brusquely than he meant to.

Laurie stepped back and rested her hand on Marion's shoulder. 'I'm so sorry, Marion.' She looked around the powdered kitchen. 'I'll clean up, honest, I will.'

But Marion shook her head firmly. 'Forget it.

You've done enough this morning.' She gave her an unexpected wink. 'Anyway, you'll not clean to my standards. June and I will manage.'

Callan shook his head. 'Marion, if you needed help in the kitchen, why didn't you let me know? I could have tried to get you some extra help for the weekend.'

He was cursing himself inside. He should have planned ahead. But the truth was, he'd been so angry about the whole scenario—the whole some-stranger-will-inherit-Annick-Castle—that he hadn't properly considered the staff there.

He knew they'd been catered for in Angus's will. But that wasn't the same. That wasn't the same as considering the pressure they would be under this weekend, or the way they would feel about having to deal with a whole host of strangers—one of whom could become their new potential boss. It wasn't just the twelve potential inheritors—some of them had brought husbands or wives with them, then there was the Murder Mystery Weekend staff too.

It wasn't like him to be so blinkered. He hated

that he hadn't considered the people he'd been amongst for years.

But Marion didn't seem so bothered. It was odd. For as long as he'd known her she'd been prickly and difficult. As if a little invisible force field stopped those around her from getting too close.

The laughing he'd heard a few moments ago had been the first he'd heard her laugh like that in years. She had a twinkle in her eye. Laurie Jenkins was currently digging her way under that force field. And he'd no idea how she'd managed it.

Marion tilted her chin, a stern look in her eye. The kitchen was her domain. 'Let me manage things in here, Callan.' Her hand swept towards the table at the far end of the kitchen. 'Laurie seems to be managing fine. She's done a good job.'

He tried not to flinch. Praise indeed from Marion and he followed her gaze to three cakes covered with glass domes and protected from the flour attack, sitting on the far-away table.

He walked over. 'You made these?' It didn't

matter that he tried to hide his surprise, the rise in inclination of his voice was a dead giveaway.

He felt Laurie appear at his side, their arms almost touching. She was smiling. She looked happy—no, she looked relaxed. The first time she'd appeared that way since she'd got here. 'Strawberry sponge, orange-iced gingerbread and flapjacks for Mr Allergy.'

He raised his eyebrows. 'Mr Allergy?'

She waved her hand. 'Don't ask. I think a pop music diva has a shorter list of demands than he has.'

He wrinkled his nose. 'So, if you've made all these, what's with the flour?'

She smiled. 'I was going to make a chocolate cake for dessert tonight.'

'Aren't you supposed to be taking part in the Murder Mystery Weekend?'

His head was spinning. Surely, the whole point of coming here was to see if she could be the potential inheritor of Annick Castle. Everything had been clearly spelled out in the letter. Why on earth was she wasting her time in the kitchen?

'Yeah, well, I suppose so.' Her eyes fixed on the

gardens outside, drifting away to her own little world. What was the story about Laurie Jenkins?

There it was. That little flicker on her face. Did she even know that happened? That little glimmer that looked a lot like hope. Right now it was fixated on the rainbow explosion that was the rose flower beds outside. Usually the castle gardens had regimented colours, red in one, pink in another, yellow and white in others. But this year he suspected Bert the gardener had fallen foul of his own poor eyesight.

Nothing had been mentioned. Nothing had been said. And the effect was actually startling. An explosion of colour right outside the kitchen windows.

Laurie turned to face him. 'To be honest I was hoping to take a walk around the gardens today.' She hesitated. 'You've already shown me the maze—how about the rest of the gardens? Isn't there a swan pond?'

Callan nodded automatically. 'Aren't you supposed to take part in all the designated activities?'

She shrugged. 'I'll make an excuse. As long as

I hand in my card at the end saying who I think the murderer is, I don't suppose it will matter. Anyway, I'll be there for dinner tonight.'

She really didn't care. She really didn't want to take part.

He was astonished. Did she know what she was giving up?

But Laurie was peering out of the window again, across the gardens to the wall next to the sea that was lined with cannons. 'Can we get down on the beach from here?'

He nodded. 'It's not the easiest path.'

'I think I'll manage.' She'd lifted one eyebrow at him, as if daring him to imply anything otherwise.

He wasn't sure whether to be angry or intrigued.

The whole purpose of the weekend was to find out who would inherit the castle. Laurie was a lawyer. Maybe she'd found a loophole in all this and knew she could mount a legal challenge. The thought sent a prickle across his skin.

He'd been assured that no matter how crazy

this whole scheme appeared, legally it was watertight—whether he liked it or not.

But that would be an explanation as to why she didn't really want to engage with the Murder Mystery Weekend. Why she wanted to spend her time exploring the estate. Maybe she was already drawing up plans in her head about what she wanted to do with the place, or how to sell it off for the highest profit.

'Callan?' Her voice was quiet and her hand rested gently on his.

His mind was running away with him again. Every time he thought about this place or the people in it, his mind naturally went for the worst-case scenario.

He looked down, trying to ignore the warmth spreading up his arm. She was looking up at him with her smudged nose and hair and her big brown eyes. Questioning the fact that for a few minutes he'd been lost in a world of his own.

There was still a light dusting of flour across the pink shoulders of her shirt. Her dark brown hair was swept up in a clasp, with stray strands escaping. The flour was like the first fall of snow at the start of winter.

She blinked, her cheeks flushing a little as he continued to stare. Her head tilted to the side. 'What time can we meet?' she prompted.

He started. Meet. Yes. That was what he was supposed to be doing.

'Half an hour.' His words came out automatically. 'I'll meet you in the entrance hall.'

She gave a little nod of her head and disappeared through the kitchen door.

Callan stared at his hand. The skin that she'd touched felt on fire. He couldn't understand. It just didn't figure.

Laurie just didn't figure.

A movement caught his eye. Marion was staring at him with her arms folded across her chest.

'What?' The words snapped out, louder than intended.

She gave him a little knowing smile, then turned her back and started busying herself around the kitchen.

For the first time, in a long time, Callan felt unnerved. And he couldn't quite work out why.

# CHAPTER FIVE

LAURIE WASN'T QUITE sure why her stomach was
churning, but it was. She frowned at her reflec-
tion in the floor-length mirror. Red Capri pants
probably weren't the most appropriate for a cliff-
side clamber but that was the trouble with travelling light. Thank goodness Marion had found
her a pair of wellington boots, and they even
matched her trousers.

She took a deep breath, grabbed her jacket and
headed along the corridor towards the stairs. The
phone in her pocket beeped and she pulled it out.
Work.

Her stomach sank like a stone. Funny how a
simple text could have that effect on her. A missing file. On a Saturday. She glanced at her watch.
If she'd been in London right now she'd probably
have been in work too. How sad was that? She
couldn't help but glance at the mysterious woman

in the portrait at the top of the stairs. Was it possible that her glare was even more disapproving than normal, and even more focused on Laurie?

She wondered if this castle had any ghosts. She'd need to ask Callan about that later. She tapped out a quick reply with a number of locations for the missing file.

As she reached the bottom of the curved staircase Robin, the Murder Mystery Weekend coordinator, rushed over, clipboard in hand. 'Ms Jenkins, I didn't see you at breakfast this morning. Was something wrong?'

Yet another person with a disapproving glare. She shrugged. 'Sorry, I was busy.'

He frowned. 'You do realise that in order to get a good idea of who the murderer is, you have to take part in all the activities.'

She bit her tongue to stop the words rolling off that she really wanted to say. It wasn't his fault Angus McLean had made this a stipulation of his will. This was just a guy doing a job.

She gave him her sweetest smile. 'Some of the activities just aren't for me.'

He looked horrified. 'But you have to take part.

You have to speak to as many of the other characters in order to build up an idea of who the murderer is.' He eyed her haughtily. 'And they need the opportunity to speak to you too.'

She sighed. 'Listen, you and I know that I'm not the murderer, so it doesn't really matter whether the other "characters"—' she lifted her fingers in the air '—speak to me or not. As long as I tell you at the end who I think is the guilty party, everything will work out fine.'

'Ms Jenkins, you're really not entering into the spirit of things. It spoils things for all the other participants too.'

She was starting to get annoyed now, and feel a little guilty, which made her even madder. She straightened herself up to her full five feet five inches. 'Well, I guess since the other participants are my new-found family, it's up to me whether I want to spend time with them or not.'

She turned and strode away as best she could in the ill-fitting red wellies. Callan was leaning against the wall next to the door with his arms folded across his chest and an amused look on his face. He pulled the main door open and picked up a jacket. 'Ready?'

There was a little spark of something in his eyes and if he said something smart right now she would take one of these wellies off and hit him over the head with it.

'Ready.' She barely turned her head as she walked straight out of the door and onto the gravel courtyard.

This place was driving her crazy.

She spun around, hands on her hips, and Callan nearly walked straight into her.

'What kind of person was Angus McLean?'

He started. 'What?'

'What kind of person was Angus McLean? Was he some kind of sick sadist that would try and pitch his unknown relatives against each other for some kind of pleasure? Did he actually think anyone would agree to this?' Now the words were coming out she couldn't stop them. 'Was he sane? Did a doctor check him over after he wrote that mad will?'

Callan hesitated for the tiniest second, then obviously thought better of getting into an unwinnable fight with an angry woman. He put his arm around her shoulders and steered her in the direction of the stairs, leading down to the impeccable gardens, fountain and maze. Her feet moved without her even really realising it, the weight of his arm behind her just making her flow along with his body. Before she knew it she was guided along to the bench in front of the trickling fountain.

Callan nudged her to sit down and she did. With a thump.

It was as if all her frustration was coming out at once.

Callan waited for a few minutes, letting them sit in silence and listen to the peaceful trickle of the fountain.

It was a beautiful setting. The bronze fairy was spouting the water from her mouth, through her hands. The water flowed down into the round pond with a mosaic bottom of blue and green tiles. The sun was high in the cloudless sky and the temperature was warm in the shelter of the lowered set of gardens.

Eventually Callan spoke, his voice deep and

calm. He was leaning forward, his arms resting on his knees. 'Angus McLean was completely sane. Frank Dalglish, the solicitor, was worried there might be a legal challenge to the will and made sure that Angus was examined by a doctor.'

'Oh.' Laurie's brain was spinning, questions firing everywhere, but Callan's voice had a real weight to it. He was completely sincere. And she realised he probably wasn't amused at her out-burst. She could smell his aftershave again, the one that seemed to play with her self-control and turn her brain to mush. Or maybe that was just the sight of his muscled arms?

'He was no sadist. And he certainly wasn't sick. Angus McLean was one of the best guys I've ever met.' He leaned back against the bench and ran his fingers through his hair, mussing it up. She liked it better that way. He shook his head. 'Truth is, Laurie, I don't understand any of this any more than you do. I spent twenty-five years around Angus McLean. I never suspected for a second that he had children. I could never under-stand why he wouldn't sell me the place. He kept telling me he wanted to keep it in the family—but as far as I knew, there wasn't any.'

He was upset. He was hurting. No matter what her thoughts were on Angus McLean she had to try and remember that this was someone who had been dear to Callan. His experience was totally different from hers.

Something registered in her brain. She looked up at the castle.

It was hard to believe but as a potential inheritor of Annick Castle she hadn't even given a moment's thought to how much it could actually be worth.

She gulped. The figures dancing around her brain made her mind boggle. She turned to face him. 'How on earth could you afford to buy a place like this?' She held up her hands. 'I have no idea how much Annick Castle would cost, but what kind of job do you have?'

She couldn't even begin to understand how someone could make enough money to buy Annick Castle. Her question probably seemed cheeky, but she was the kind of girl who usually said what came to mind. And she wasn't going to stop just because she was here.

'If I tell you will you be able to reply in one hundred and fifty characters or less?'

It took a few seconds for the penny to drop. She couldn't help it; her mouth fell open.

'You? You own Blether?' She couldn't believe it. The Scottish equivalent of Twitter, with a slightly longer letter count, had started as a rival company six or seven years before. It had taken the advertising market by storm. Those ten little letters made all the difference, but still allowed short, sharp messages.

He gave a rueful smile and nodded. 'Guilty as charged. I owned an Internet search engine before that. Blether came about almost by accident.'

She was stunned. Everyone knew exactly how successful the company was, but she'd never really heard anything about the owner. 'How so?'

'I was annoyed one night and came home and spouted off to Angus about it. He told me to stop bellyaching and do something about it. He challenged me to make something bigger and better.'

She shook her head. 'And the name?'

He shrugged. 'How could it have been anything else? Blether—the Scots word for people who talk incessantly.' He raised his eyebrows at her. 'You should be able to relate.'

Her reaction was automatic; she elbowed him in the ribs. 'Cheeky.'

They sat quietly for a few more seconds as she tried to take in everything he'd just told her. He must be worth millions—no, probably billions—and here he was, sitting at Annick Castle for a crazy Murder Mystery Weekend. It just didn't make sense.

'So, your background is in computers, then?'

He shook his head. 'It should be, but it isn't. I did pure mathematics at university.'

'You did?'

He smiled and looked up at the castle. She could see the fondness in his eyes, see the memories flit across his face. 'I wasn't doing too well at school before I met Angus. My father didn't believe in homework. And as a child I had other skills that were my priority.'

Something about the way he said the words sent a chill down her spine. He hadn't emphasised them, or been too explicit, but it was almost as if the skills he was hinting at were survival skills.

'Once I started spending time with Angus he used to sit me down at the kitchen table at night and go over my homework with me. He was methodical—and strict. He discovered I had a natural aptitude for maths and he bought me text-books and journals that challenged me.'

'So you did your homework here?' It seemed the safest question to ask, without prying too much.

'Pretty much. Angus helped me with my exams. He even helped me fill in my applica-tion for university.'

'Where did you go?'

'I got into Cambridge—and Oxford, but in the end I went to Edinburgh. I didn't want to leave Scotland.'

'You didn't?' She didn't mean to sound so sur-prised; it just came out that way. It hadn't even occurred to her for a second to turn down her university place at Cambridge. Did people actu-ally do that? And how distracted would she have been if she'd met Callan at university?

He stood up and arched his back, obviously trying to relieve some tension. 'Look around you, Laurie. What's not to love?'

It was the way he said the words. So simple. Without a second thought.

And she did look around her.

At the magnificent sand-coloured castle looking out over the Scottish coastline.

At the immaculate maze.

At the colourful, impeccably kept gardens.

At the forest and vegetation around them, set against the start of a mountain range.

It was almost as if something sucked the air out of her lungs.

She lived her life in London. She spent her day jumping on and off the tube, breathing in other people's air. She was surrounded by high-rise buildings and streets that often never saw any sunlight. Continual fights over parking spaces, and eternally rising rents.

She didn't have a single friend in London that had a garden. Her own flat had a window box that she rarely filled with flowering shrubs—on the few occasions that she had she often forgot to water them.

She couldn't remember the last time she'd walked on grass. How long had it been since she'd gone to Hyde Park?

'You want me to tell you a little of the history of the place?'

She nodded. She knew absolutely nothing about Annick Castle.

Callan sat back on the bench, resting his arm along the back as she settled next to him. His arm was brushing the top of her shoulders. It was as if a whole host of butterflies were flapping their wings against her skin. 'The castle was built originally in the fifteen-hundreds.' There was a gleam in his eyes. 'There's even a rumour that Mary Queen of Scots once stayed here. It was enlarged, rebuilt and the gardens planted in the seventeen-hundreds. The Earl of Annick's family owned the estate for years. They were connected to the Kennedy family in Scotland who can trace their ancestry back to Robert the Bruce. In later years they had connections with some of the most powerful families in America.'

'I had no idea. So how did the castle end up in the hands of Angus McLean?'

'There were a number of properties like this all over Scotland. Some of them were poorly maintained because of the costs involved, others just weren't lived in all year round. In 1945 a lot of them were handed over to the National Trust in Scotland. But this one had caught the eye of Angus's father—he owned a pharmaceutical company and was about the only person who hadn't gone bankrupt after the Second World War. He bought the place for a song.'

Laurie let a hiss of air out through her lips. Maybe not this castle, but something had been here for five hundred years. It was amazing. All that history in one place.

She could be sitting in the same place that Mary Queen of Scots had once stood.

Callan had reached out his hand towards her and she took it without question, letting him pull her up from the bench. Warmth encapsulated her hand. There was a chilly breeze coming off the sea and part of her wished he would wrap her in his arms.

'Come on,' he said. 'You wanted to see the grounds. Let's go down to the swan pond.'

She followed him along the gravel path, winding past the fountain and flower beds. Small things started to prick her mind. Some of the plants here were a little wilder, a little less trimmed. The bushes weren't quite as shaped as the ones underneath the castle windows.

'Who looks after the grounds, Callan?'

He turned, his hand gesturing towards another set of steps. 'Bert mostly. He has a few of the local boys who come and help him, but he generally scares them all off within a few months.' He pointed back at the perfect green lawn. 'Last year Angus persuaded him to let another company come in and cut the lawns and do the edging.' He rolled his eyes. 'You've no idea the fight that caused.' There was a real affection in his voice.

She walked down the steps that were sheltered by some thick foliage. When she reached the bottom she let out a little gasp. She turned to face Callan. 'When you said swan pond I was thinking of something much smaller.'

He gave a nod and a smile. 'Some people don't

even know it exists. The castle grounds are sheltered and on an incline. It means that you have to walk down steps at each level.' They walked closer to the edge of the pond. It was the size of around four football pitches and Laurie could see a few white swans bobbing in the middle.

'What's that over there?' There was an elegant glass and white metal gazebo on the other side of the pond. 'It looks as if you lifted it straight out of *The Sound of Music* and put it there.'

Callan nodded. 'What if I told you it had a bench that ran all the way around the inside?'

'Really?' Her stomach gave a little flutter. Her mind instantly had her inside the gazebo with Callan twirling her around in his arms. The chemistry between them seemed to increase the more time she spent with him; it was getting hard not to acknowledge it. Did Callan think so too?

She wasn't sure. He nodded and gave her a half-smile. 'Really. It's just coincidence. It's more than a hundred years old. Angus's parents had it built. The swan pond was his mother's favourite spot, but she didn't like sitting in the sun.'

'It's gorgeous. Can we go around?'

He glanced at his watch. 'Maybe later. We've still got a lot of ground to cover.'

Laurie glanced down at her footwear. If she was going to visit the castle's own *Sound of Music* gazebo she didn't really want to do it in red wellies. It kind of spoiled the mood. 'Okay, then, where to next?'

Callan led her up another set of steps that took them around the other side of the castle. They passed outbuildings that looked a little worse for wear. A set of unused stables and a round stone building that was almost falling down.

The stonework on this side of the castle wasn't as clean as the front and there were a number of slates on the ground. Were they from the roof?

The round building was fascinating and she couldn't help but go and peer through the doorway. 'What was this?'

'It was one of the old icehouses on the estate. They used to cut ice from the swan pond and store it here for use in the house. The old icehouses were the forerunners of refrigeration. And watch out—you probably need a hard hat to go in there.'

'Wow. What other buildings are there?'

'As well as the gazebo at the swan pond, there is an orangery. It was built in 1818. It was used later as a camellia house and had one-inch-thick glass, a dome top and a furnace at the back of the building to supply under-floor heating. They used to think that delicate flowers needed to be grown in hothouses. There also used to be a pagoda overlooking the swan pond, but it fell into ruins—only the foundations are left now.'

This place was truly amazing—she didn't even know the half of it. No wonder Callan loved it so much. 'What was that for?'

'The lower level was the swan house and aviary with the gazebo or teahouse above. During its time the aviary housed specimens of gold and silver pheasants, pigeons of fancy varieties, kites and hunting hawk. It's also thought that one time a monkey was housed here, giving the pagoda its local nickname of the "monkey house".'

She shook her head. 'I had no idea the estate was so big.' She was also astounded at Callan's knowledge and the way everything just tripped off his tongue. 'Did you ever see it?'

He wrinkled his brow. 'It was partially standing when I was a boy. There was still some glass and stone remaining. And there's more. There are old gatehouses, a water house and a gas house all around the grounds of the estate. There's an old dairy, a stonemason's and another set of stables.'

Laurie had no idea about any of this. When she'd done the Internet search for Annick Castle, she'd only really looked at the pictures of the actual castle. She hadn't read up on how big the estate was or what it contained.

They'd reached the wall again that looked out over the sea. She placed her hands on her hips and looked around her. 'This place is just amazing.' She sighed.

'Yeah. It is.' Callan had that look again, the one where he just drifted off and she couldn't help but wonder what was going on in his head.

She cleared her throat. 'I hope you don't mind me saying, but parts of it look a little...run-down.'

He didn't hesitate. 'I know. You're right. I tried to speak to Angus about it for the last few years.

But I've got no control over what happens on the estate, and I had no right to order repairs—even though I was willing to pay for some of them myself.'

'He didn't want to maintain the castle?' It sounded odd. And she couldn't imagine why.

Callan leaned back against the wall. 'He just grew old—and stubborn. And he wouldn't let me help him with his finances.' He shrugged his shoulders. 'I was worried he didn't actually have any money left. He still had his faculties but his decision-making processes, well—they just seemed to disintegrate.'

'And yet he still managed to make the strangest will in the world?'

'There's no cure for old age, Laurie.' He gave a nod towards the next set of steps. 'Come on. Let's put those wellies to good use.'

He removed a thin piece of rope closing off the steps and started down them. Laurie made to follow and stopped dead. It wasn't a traditional set of steps. They were precarious, cut into the cliff side with only a thread rope as a handhold. At places they looked almost vertical.

Callan moved down them easily, sure-footed without a second's hesitation. He made it look easy.

Except it was far from easy.

'Come on,' he shouted over his shoulder. 'If you fall you'll only land on me.'

Part of his confidence annoyed her—which was silly. He'd lived here for a good part of his life. He could probably go down these steps with his eyes shut.

Venturing down them in a pair of somebody else's ill-fitting wellies was an entirely different story. In some ways she might have taken great pleasure in landing squarely between his shoulders. In another, despite his bravado, it was likely they would both tumble down the cliff face and land in the rocks below. Quite frankly, she wasn't that brave.

She took her time as she edged down the steps, shouting down to Callan in an attempt to appear casual, 'You never told me, how did you end up going from pure mathematics to computers?'

He was so far beneath her now. The noise from

the crashing waves below almost drowned out his reply. 'Boredom, or luck, I guess.'

She took the next few steps a little quicker. She was becoming more sure-footed, the thin rope slipping easily through her fingers. She knew her brow was wrinkled as she took the last few steps towards him. 'I don't get it. Boredom? Whoops—'

The last few steps were slicked with moss and lichens, the thick soles of the wellies having hardly any grip at all. His hands planted firmly on her hip bones, stopping her from losing her balance completely.

She was one step above him, meaning they were almost face-to-face.

If the breath hadn't exited her lungs so quickly she might have smiled. The view was good here.

Any woman would tell you that from first glance Callan McGregor was a fine figure of a man. But this close she could see everything— his slightly tanned, slightly weathered skin. The smattering of tiny freckles across his nose. Her hands had lifted to stop her falling and were now naturally placed on the breadth of his chest. After a few seconds she could feel the heat from his skin seeping through his cotton shirt onto the palms of her hands.

She should move them. She really should. But right now they felt superglued to his chest.

She caught her breath. 'Boredom?' she asked softly.

They were so close now the crashing waves were merely background noise. He hadn't moved his hands; they were still firmly on her hips, steering her closer to him.

He blinked. If he'd been any closer those long eyelashes of his might have brushed her cheek. She shouldn't feel so comfortable. Under normal circumstances she would have jumped back, hating her personal space being invaded without her say-so.

But nothing about this weekend had been normal. Why change anything now?

From this position she had a real clear view of his green eyes. Bright green eyes. Unlike any she'd seen before. There was nothing pale or wishy-washy about them. She'd seen an emerald this green once before on the jewellery shopping channel. Was it from Colombia? It had been three carats, with a single carat diamond on either side. Probably the most gorgeous ring she'd ever seen and well out of her price range. Funny how the billionaire's eyes reminded her of that.

He tilted his head to one side. 'Just because I had a natural talent for maths didn't mean I had to spend my life doing it.'

He said it as if it made perfect sense.

A gust of wind swept past her, pushing her even closer to him. Every hair on her arms stood on end. But it wasn't the wind. It was him. His touch. And his words. Doing a whole host of strange things to her.

It was more than unsettling. She tried to pull her tongue down from its current position of sticking to the roof of her mouth. It wasn't often in this life that Laurie found it difficult to talk.

'But what did Angus say? Didn't he tell you to find a career related to your degree?' She'd already realised there was no point asking what his father thought. He hadn't even mentioned his mother at all. And she couldn't ask the question that was throbbing in her head right now: *What would my father have thought if I'd walked away from law?* Because neither Callan nor she would know the answer.

Callan smiled. A smile that reached right up into those green eyes. Little wrinkles appeared around them. Good wrinkles. He looked so much better when he smiled rather than the permanent frown that had been on his face since she'd met him.

'Angus would never have told me to do something that made me unhappy. I'd completed my degree. It was up to me to find my place in life.'

He said the words so easily. As if it was the way it should be for everyone and she felt her stomach twist in tight knots.

Why couldn't she have said something like that to her father? Only hers hadn't been an ordinary kind of degree. What else could you do with a law degree if you didn't practise law? Sure, there were some students in her class who hadn't gone on to complete their professional qualifications after sitting their exams. They'd moved into other professions.

But she wasn't exactly sure what. Truth was,

she'd been too scared to pay too much attention to any other options. It had almost been easier to work on the assumption that there was none. She would never have disappointed her father. She just couldn't have.

Horrible things were jumping around in her mind. What would have happened if she'd told her father that she didn't like her degree? What would have happened if he'd still been alive and she'd told him she hated her job? She could feel tears prickling in the backs of her eyes. All of a sudden she felt cold. Really cold. Did this make her a coward?

'Laurie?' Callan's voice was quiet; she could feel his warm breath on her cheek, see his eyes full of concern.

'But what if you can't find your place in life?' she whispered. *Or, you're too scared to.*

She was going to cry, any second now she was going to burst into tears, on the edge of the Scottish coastline with a virtual stranger.

Callan didn't say a word. He slipped his arm around her shoulders, holding her close to his side, and guided her down the last few steps onto the thin line of shingle beach. Judging from the moss and lichen on the shingles, this part of the coastline must regularly be underwater.

The warmth from his body was comforting. The feel of the arm around her shoulder was reassuring—protective almost. He hadn't asked her any questions. It was almost as if he knew she was upset and he sensed not to push her.

They walked a few hundred yards along the coastline and he stopped at the rock face. 'Look,' he said, his mouth brushing against her ear.

She lifted her head. Carved into the rocks in front of her were three arches—as if someone had tried to create a house out of one of the natural caves. The arches were on three levels, almost as if it had been someone's home.

'What on earth is this?' It was a perfect distraction. So unusual, and so mysterious that she couldn't help but ask the question and push the other heavy thoughts from her mind.

'Welcome to the history of Annick Castle. This part of the coast was a notorious centre for smuggling and the fortified caves beneath the castle were ideal for hiding contraband from the Revenue Officers. For centuries the Annick Kennedys and others on the estate were either directly involved in smuggling, or turned a blind eye to it, in exchange for a share of the profits.'

'No.' Laurie felt her eyes grow wide. 'Really?' This was fascinating to her. A whole part of her family history she knew nothing about. 'So, you're telling me my relatives were involved in smuggling?'

Callan smiled as they entered the cave. 'It seems that way. This was all long before Angus's time, but it is amazing, isn't it? And it's part of the heritage of Annick Castle.'

He sounded a little wistful as he said those words. They stood for a moment in the cave. It wasn't quite as dark as she'd thought, the carved windows letting in lots of light. It was damp and slimy, with the water lapping around her wellies. There was a ledge high above her at the second window.

Laurie pointed. 'I take it the contraband had to be moved up there at high tide?'

Callan shrugged. 'I would assume so.' He walked over and touched one of the walls. 'Just imagine if these walls could talk. What do you think they would tell us?'

She walked over and laid her hand on the damp, cold wall next to his. 'How many of those smugglers died on the rocks out there? This doesn't look like the easiest bit of coast to navigate—not that I know anything about sailing.'

Callan nodded. 'That's a good point. This is a pretty treacherous part of the coast. Even today, sailing around here isn't really encouraged. I can remember a few wrecks over the years.' He gave a little smile. 'When I was a young boy I spent most of my time down here fighting imaginary pirates.'

She could almost imagine him dressed up with a pretend sword, swooping in and out of the atmospheric cave. 'Was it safe to play down here?'

He laughed. 'I take it these days it would need a whole health and safety check before anyone set foot on those steps. But when I was young Angus could always tell me the tide tables. As long as it wasn't high tide, I was allowed to come and play.' He gave her a measured look. 'Do you think you would have come and joined me?'

The question took her by surprise. A million thoughts and possibilities had floated around her head. What if Angus McLean had made contact with her dad years ago? What if she'd had a chance to spend summers here—to spend summers playing in *The Sound of Music* gazebo, pretending to be Liesl? What if she'd had a chance to grow up around Callan McGregor?

She pushed the thought from her mind and met his smile. 'I was a girl's girl. Pirates and damp caves would have horrified me. I guess, as every little girl would, I would have dreamed of being a fairy princess in the castle. To be honest, I would probably have spent most of my time sweeping up and down that fabulous staircase. Hours of fun presenting myself at the ball.' She gave an imaginary curtsey. He went to speak but she raised her finger. 'But as a teenager, I would have put a no-fly zone around the gazebo and spent every evening re-enacting the dancing scene, singing "Sixteen Going on Seventeen" with the gentleman of my choice.'

Callan raised his eyebrows. 'And who might that have been?'

He moved a little closer. Or did she just imagine it?

Nope. His fingers had definitely edged nearer hers on the wall. 'That all depends.'

'Depends on what?'

His voice had grown quieter, huskier. It was sending shivers down her spine and her body was reacting in the most natural manner—moving even closer to hear his words.

'Depends on who the hero of the moment was.' It was the perfect time to tease him. And she had to tease him. Because otherwise she might end up wishing for something else entirely. 'When I was sixteen I went through a real retro phase—I loved Marty McFly from *Back to the Future*. I wanted him to magically appear in his DeLorean and take me off. By seventeen I'd moved on completely and thought I would marry a member of Take That.'

Callan cringed. 'Save me from boy bands!'

She shook her head. 'It was downhill all the way from there. I still had a tiny bit of retro films going on. Indiana Jones was definitely my overall favourite.'

He raised his eyes. 'So, no pirates?' His eyes were darker in here. He was standing with his back to the incoming light, making his pupils even bigger.

It was easy to imagine what film he was talking about now. She smiled. 'No, funnily enough, pirates never did it for me.'

He blinked. Thick, dark lashes over bright green eyes nearly obliterated by the huge pupils. 'Pity.'

He said the word so quietly it was almost a whisper. But it was the hidden implication. The expression on his face. Laurie was frozen. She couldn't move. No, she didn't want to move.

She knew exactly what he was thinking. Because her mind was in the same place.

She was in the same position as earlier. Inches away from Callan McGregor. Except this time she wasn't standing on a set of exposed steps; this time she was standing in a darkened cave.

Any second now he might move closer. She couldn't help it. Her lips felt instantly dry and she ran her tongue along them.

He lifted his hand and her breath caught in

her throat. Was he going to kiss her? But no. He reached up and touched a long brown curl, pushing it back over her shoulder. 'You're a strange one, Laurie Jenkins.'

She tilted her head to the side. 'What do you mean?'

He sighed. 'I mean, I haven't found you stealing the family silver. You don't seem that interested in the Murder Mystery Weekend, but you *do* seem really interested in the castle.'

'That's because I am.' It was the simplest answer because it was true. It was cold in here. If she just inched forward a little...

'But why? Because of how much it will be worth if you inherit it?'

His words sounded harsh. And they offended her. She pulled back.

'Is that what you think?'

Callan hadn't moved his eyes from hers. 'That's just it, Laurie—I'm not sure what I think.'

She moved a little backwards. His gaze was starting to unnerve her. But she was determined to speak her mind.

'I want the opportunity to meet other members

of my so-called family. I'm still not sure how I feel about all this. Most of the time it makes me angry. You talk about Angus McLean with great affection, Callan, but for me—he's just some unknown guy that ignored his children. I can't get my head round that at all.' She lifted her hands up. 'And this, a castle, spectacular grounds, caves and a history just waiting to be learned. It's more than I could ever have imagined. I'm trying to decide how much I want to be part of all this— if at all.'

His expression changed quickly. He looked almost scornful. 'You mean you don't want to inherit the castle?'

She shook her head. He really didn't understand her at all. And she wasn't even sure she could put it into words. She could barely understand it herself. 'I mean, I don't know what I would do with it, Callan. Look at me.' She put her hand on her chest. 'I'm a London girl from a small family. I'm a lawyer. What do I know about castles? I've never seen anything like this before. How on earth would I fit in? You've had the benefit of being here since you were young. You grew up here. You know everything there is to know—'

'Or not.' His words were quick. She'd forgotten Angus hadn't told him about his children either. This must be even harder for him than it was for her.

He'd cut off her frustration mid-sentence. And she just couldn't find the words to continue. She needed some time. She needed some time to get her head around all this.

She took a deep breath in the vain hope it would fill her lungs and straighten out her head.

Work. Getting away from work had been the first step for her.

The letter and invite to Annick Castle had been the starting point in the process, but now she was away and out of her usual environment she was scared of how she was feeling. She was scared by how much she was embracing things, relishing the change and enjoying little things she would never usually experience.

She was scared of the horrible feeling in the pit of her stomach when she realised she would have to board a train in a few days to head back down to London.

Back to the long hours, aching muscles and tension headaches. Back to a life that revolved completely around work. She'd long since abandoned her gym membership after she'd only found the time to go twice. Was that what she really wanted?

The waves started to lap in around her feet. Callan looked down. 'Time to go. The tide comes in quite slowly at this time of day. We've got around twenty minutes to get up the steps.'

He strode out of the cave into the bright sunlight while Laurie stood for a few seconds longer.

She took a deep breath. What was she doing? She had no idea who Callan McGregor was. Every time she was around him she was unsettled.

She couldn't help but feel a tiny bit envious of the fact he'd grown up here.

She couldn't help but feel even more envious that Angus never had any expectation of him beyond going to university.

She squeezed her eyes tightly shut. This was

disloyal. She wasn't even going to allow herself to think like that.

It was time to get a hold of herself. Time to stop with the crazy thoughts and focus on the reason she was here—to try and get to know her family members.

She lifted her head and walked back outside into the sunlight.

# CHAPTER SIX

'KNOCK, KNOCK.'

Callan cringed. He'd recognise that high-pitched voice anywhere. It was Robin, the Murder Mystery Weekend organiser. It didn't matter where in the castle he tried to hide, the guy seemed to have an inbuilt antenna and could find him anyway.

Robin stuck his head around the door. 'Dinner will be served in ten minutes. We were hoping you would have made it to the pre-dinner drinks. You did agree to participate.' There it was. That tiny disapproving edge to his voice that he seemed to have in every conversation with Callan. It was almost as if he were an eighty-year-old grumpy headmaster trapped inside a gangly twenty-five-year-old's body.

Callan tried not to say what he was really thinking. He stared at the crumpled piece of card he'd been given earlier with his instructions. They included *Flirt with Lucy Clark, get into an argument with Philippe Deveraux*. No problem. If the man was drunk again and put his hands on Laurie he'd do more than argue with him.

Where had that come from? The thought surprised him. He'd only known the woman two days and already she was getting under his skin.

Who was he kidding?

She'd probably got under his skin from the second the smoke had cleared at the railway station and he'd caught sight of the curvy brunette. But when they'd been standing on the steps earlier and he could see her brown eyes filled with tears he couldn't help but feel protective towards her. Something was going on with Laurie Jenkins— and it was nothing to do with inheriting a castle. The question was, did he really want to find out?

Did he want to get to know any of Angus's relatives who were milling around the place he thought of as his home? Once one of them inherited it, he would have to clear out his things and start staying in his Edinburgh town house.

And even though he owned a beautiful home he couldn't bear the thought of that.

The place he called home was here.

'Callan, can I count on you?'

Robin. He'd forgotten he was even there. He gave the organiser a quick nod and watched him scuttle off.

Callan closed his computer. He was doing exactly what he'd been dreading. Examining the castle accounts. In the interim period between Angus dying and the castle being handed over he'd been appointed as caretaker. The upkeep of the castle was huge. Heating, lighting and maintenance costs were astronomical. The roof needed some repairs. They needed to employ more staff to help Bert with the grounds. Whoever inherited Annick Castle was going to get a nasty shock.

A horrible little coil of guilt was snaking around him. He should have stepped in earlier. He should have spoken to Angus about how run-down parts of the estate were becoming.

But the truth was he had too much respect for Angus to ever have done that.

But maybe there was a little hope. Maybe if he

made more of an effort to talk to the relatives he could plant the seeds about how costly the castle would be. With any luck he could put in a generous offer and buy the castle, just as he'd always wanted to.

It seemed mercenary. It seemed calculating. But none of these people felt the way he did about the castle. The only one who'd shown any real interest in anything other than its retail value was Laurie, and even she'd admitted that she'd be out of her depth.

He picked up the jacket that was sitting on the Louis XV armchair. It was the same one he'd worn the night before. He'd no idea whose idea it had been that all the guests should dress in 1920s clothes but this was as far as he'd go.

He could hear the noise in the main drawing room as he descended the stairs, some laughter louder than others.

He saw Laurie as soon as he entered the room. She was sitting next to another woman on one of the red velvet chaises longues. It was Mary, from Ireland, the one aunt that she'd really wanted to talk to.

She was wearing an emerald-green dress with beading around the scooped neckline. It skirted the top of her knees and she had a matching pair of shoes. Her hair was swept back on one side with an elaborate clasp made of jewels and blue and green feathers. Was that a peacock? He couldn't help but smile.

The dress could have been made specifically for her. It skimmed her curves, hinting at them without giving too much away. The dress colour accentuated the light tan of her skin and the glossy chestnut of her hair that hung in curls around one shoulder. She'd applied some heavier make-up, her eyes outlined in kohl and her lips red and glossy. It was all he could do to stop himself staring at them.

But what he noticed most about her was how animated she seemed. She was clutching a photograph in one hand that she'd obviously been showing to her aunt and the two of them were talking at once. Her eyes were sparkling, her other hand gesturing frequently, and her aunt Mary seemed equally engaged.

Laurie was the only person in the room he was

interested in talking to, but he couldn't disturb them. He walked over to the sideboard where a vast array of drinks was laid out. He didn't for a second imagine that any of the bottles had been half empty when they'd been put out, but most of them were well on their way to being finished.

He poured himself some soda water and gritted his teeth. He did drink alcohol himself—in moderation. But he hated being around people that were drunk. Having an alcoholic as a father did that to you. When his father had succumbed to alcoholic liver disease a few years ago Callan had actually felt a sigh of relief. It was as if he could finally shake off that part of his life.

He looked around the room again. He was still finding it hard to get his head around the fact that he was surrounded by Angus's relatives—Angus's *family*. Twelve people who'd never had a single conversation with Angus McLean in their lives, one of whom could inherit the thing he'd held most dear. No matter which way he looked at it, it still didn't make sense.

But as much as he didn't want to admit it, he was noticing a few similarities in some of the guests. Two of the sons definitely looked like Angus—one so much so that Marion had commented it was like being around a younger version of him.

One of his daughters had identical blue twinkling eyes and a dimple in her right cheek. He couldn't see any physical similarities in any of the other relatives.

Family. Why hadn't Angus surrounded himself with these people?

He'd never really understood the whole 'Annick Castle should be kept in the family' ethos and had questioned Angus about it on more than one occasion.

But Angus had made comments about family on other continents. Callan's problem was he'd imagined that was some distant far-flung second cousin who'd eventually inherit the castle. He'd always had the thought at the back of his mind the said cousin wouldn't want to move continent and change their life, so would be happy with a financial offer instead.

But he hadn't imagined this. He hadn't imagined children.

It made it all so much more personal.

He watched as Laurie threw back her head and laughed, revealing the paler skin of her throat. It was the same hearty laugh he'd heard in the kitchen earlier. He liked it, but from the way Laurie had acted earlier today he guessed she didn't get to do it often enough.

It was as if the rest of the room just faded into oblivion whenever she was around. At least that was what happened in his head. This woman was invading every part of his senses. Even when he wasn't with her he was thinking about her, and when he *was* with her it was all he could do to keep his hands to himself.

What had she meant—*What if you can't find your place in life*? She was a lawyer living in London. She'd gone to Cambridge to do her degree. Surely she'd already found her place in life?

He knew she was successful—he'd Googled her. There didn't seem to be any bad reports about her work and the case she'd quoted the other night—about winning a client half a million pounds—had been entirely true.

And why was Laurie Jenkins intriguing him

so much? Why, when she'd looked as if she was about to burst into tears on the coastal steps, had he just wanted to put his arms around her?

Everything about her drew him in like a magnet. Her sparkiness, her ability to cut through the crap, but still have a hint of vulnerability about her. She spoke with love about her father, disappointment that he hadn't got to meet Angus McLean and she didn't try to hide her disdain that Angus hadn't met his children.

He couldn't blame her. And as much as that hurt him, part of him was pleased that she didn't tiptoe around him.

So what was it that was making Laurie Jenkins unhappy? Because he could see it. See it in her eyes when she had those fleeting moments off in a little world of her own. He could sense it in the little gaps in conversation as she tried to take in the beauty of Annick Castle and its surroundings.

All he knew was he liked it better when Laurie had a smile on her face and that twinkle in her brown eyes. He liked it better when he could hear the laughter that seemed to come from the very bottom of her soul. Just as she was now.

Her eyes met his across the room and she paused for a second, then lifted the glass of rosé she had in her hand towards him and gave him a little smile of acknowledgement.

'Dinner is served, everyone.' Robin's voice jolted him.

Callan caught Robin's steely glare clearly directed at him. Darn it. He'd forgotten about flirting with Laurie and causing an argument. To be frank it was the last thing on his mind. Flirting with Laurie he could do in a heartbeat, but the argument? He really couldn't be bothered. He'd just need to remedy that at dinner.

Laurie walked straight over to him as they entered the dining room and reached the table, her green dress swishing around her with the sway of her hips as she moved. 'I met my aunt Mary,' she said. 'And she's fabulous. It's so strange how some of her mannerisms are the same as my dad's. Even though they never met. I can't believe it.'

She glanced at the table with the name settings and promptly reached over and swapped hers with someone else's so she could sit next to Callan. He raised his eyebrows at her but she shook her head and said quietly, 'Don't want to be stuck between those two—they've spent the whole evening arguing.'

He smiled and whispered in her ear. 'Don't you think you might be spoiling the activities of the night by doing that?'

She gave him a wink. 'I'm quite capable of sorting out my own activities for the night.'

He liked it. Her cheeky side that he'd only glimpsed on a few occasions. Most of the time Laurie Jenkins was obviously on her guard around him. And who could blame her? She'd walked into a weekend full of strangers. Some of whom were friendlier than others.

'I'll bet you are,' he replied. If he thought about that too long his imagination would run riot.

'Did you speak to any of your other relatives?'

She rolled her eyes. 'Yes, and no. Mary was great. Joe from Canada was great too.' She wiggled her hand and pointed at the name cards she'd moved. 'I'm not so sure about Arnold and Audrey.'

Callan raised his eyebrows. 'Were they taking pictures while they spoke to you?'

Laurie nodded and moved to the side as her dinner plate was put in front of her, the feathers in her hairclip brushing against his face. 'Yes! And what's that little black book they continually scribble notes in? What on earth are they up to?'

She straightened up, leaving her perfume wafting around him. Something spicy, more sensual than the floral scent she'd been wearing today. It wound its way around him, prickling his senses.

He waited until all the other guests had been served, then picked up his knife and fork, trying to clear his head. Marion had got some help this evening and things certainly appeared to be going more smoothly. Like all the food that came out of her kitchen the chicken Caesar salad looked delicious. If only he could concentrate on it.

He gave her a smile. 'I hate to think what they're up to. You know I caught one of them in my rooms yesterday?'

'You're joking? Really?' Her mouth was hanging open. 'What on earth were they doing?'

He shrugged. 'I didn't wait to find out. I just shouted at them, told them my rooms were private and showed them out.'

Laurie shook her head. 'That's just ridiculous.'

'I think we should change seats.' The interruption was brisk. Callan heard the male voice in his ear and felt the hand pressing heavily on his shoulder. He resisted his first reaction. Although Craig had obviously had a bit too much to drink again this evening, Callan's instruction card for this evening had told him to flirt with Laurie's character and get into an argument with Craig, or his alter ego Philippe Deveraux. He'd paid little enough attention to the Murder Mystery Weekend without trying to wreck the one small part he'd been asked to be involved in. He would give him the benefit of the doubt. For five minutes only.

He stood up. 'I think you'll find Ms Clark has decided she wants my attention this evening.' He looked down at the dinner table. 'I think you'll also find that the entrées have already been served. Take a seat, Mr Deveraux.'

From the corner of the room he could almost

see the Murder Mystery Weekend organiser clapping his hands with glee.

Craig looked momentarily confused, then obviously realised he was supposed to be in character. 'You've monopolised Laurie—I mean, Ms Clark's attention all day. It's time to let her mix with some other company.'

Callan wondered exactly how far he was supposed to go with this. As Laurie lifted a glass of wine to her rose-red lips he had an instant spark of inspiration. Or maybe it was her scent that was still permeating his skin? Whatever it was, he reached down and pulled her to her feet.

After all, he had agreed to play along.

'I think you'll find Ms Clark is already spoken for, Mr Deveraux. I suggest you take your seat.' And at that, he bent down and brushed his lips next to Laurie's.

He felt her instantly stiffen in shock. He hadn't given her any warning. He hadn't given it much thought himself. He was just playing along and it seemed like the natural thing to do.

Bartholomew Grant would surely want to stake his claim on his girlfriend?

His hand was around her waist, supporting her as she leaned back a little. Across the table Auntie Mary burst into a round of applause.

Her lips were soft and pliable, but, oh, so inviting. He meant just to brush the slightest touch, but his lips caught the taste of wine from her and his gentle brush became instantly more intense. He felt her hands place on his chest. For an instant he wondered if she was going to push him away, but she didn't. Instead her hands rested lightly—just as they had done earlier that day on the steps.

Her scent wound its way around him, rich, sultry and exotic. It was truly intoxicating. If he didn't stop now, he never would.

Only the briefest few seconds had passed but he was conscious of the audience around them, and conscious of the fact if she did object, she might not want to do so in front of others.

He pulled back but felt her lips still connected with his. It was as if she didn't want the kiss to end. Had she felt the same connection he had? As their noses brushed against each other he opened his eyes. Her dark brown eyes were already open, staring straight at him.

She looked a little stunned. As if she didn't quite believe the kiss had happened. Her hand came up automatically to her lips, which seemed even redder, even fuller than before.

Her eyes still hadn't left his. All he could see was how chocolate-coloured they looked in this light and a definite dilation of her black pupils. His body reacted instantly—a natural response. Her hips were still pressed against his and her eyes widened, but the smile that appeared on her face was one of pure mischief.

As if on cue, one of the other guests stood up and started shouting—obviously all part of the activities. Callan stepped back, releasing his hand from around her back, and reluctantly sank back down into his seat. 'Sorry, if I took you by surprise,' he murmured.

She lifted her glass and took another sip of wine. There was a cheeky glint in her eyes. Laurie Jenkins wasn't upset or offended. Quite the opposite, in fact. It made the blood race through his body. 'Seems like it was surprises all round,' she said softly.

Up close the green dress was perfect for her skin tone and chestnut-coloured hair. Her cheeks glowed and the red gloss on her lips shined. The beads around the neckline caught the candlelight in the room and dazzled. She looked as if she belonged on a magazine cover, or an old-fashioned portrait. But here she was sitting at his side.

He wanted to sweep the rest of the guests away. He wanted to erase the Murder Mystery Weekend completely. He wanted the chance to get to know Angus McLean's granddaughter on his own, with no distractions.

But the long evening stretched ahead of them. He spoke solicitously to the other guests around him. He ate the steak placed in front of him. But all the while his eyes were watching her every move. Every sip of her wine. Every mouthful of delicious food.

Laurie knew it. And she was enjoying it. Seemed like teasing Callan was the order of the night.

The play-acting continued around them. Cal-

Ian hadn't paid attention to a single part of it. He leaned over and whispered in her ear. 'Do you have any idea who the murderer is?'

She looked up through her darkened lashes. 'Of course I do, Callan. I've known from day one. But it wouldn't be fair if I told you. You have to guess for yourself.'

'But I don't need to guess. I don't have anything to inherit.' As soon as he said the words he could feel them wash over his body like an icy wave.

It kept coming back to this. One of the people at the table would inherit the place he called home.

Part of him wanted to behave like a child. Part of him wanted to scream and shout that even though DNA might say they were related to Angus, none of them had been his family.

*He* was Angus's family.

He'd been the one to make adjustments to Angus's rooms so it was easier for him to get about. He'd been the one who'd eventually had to help him in and out of the bath and shower. He'd been the one who'd tried to persuade him to eat and drink as he'd started to fade away. He was the one that had sat by his bedside while his chest rattled night after night.

He was the one that held his hand while he died.

He was the one that shed a mountain of tears.

Not one person in this room knew a single thing about Angus. They weren't family. No matter what the DNA said.

And it made him angry.

It made him angry to see relatives examining the antiques and trying to find their value on the Internet. It made him angry to hear them discussing market values. Had they no respect?

'Callan? Are you okay?'

Laurie was looking at him with those big brown eyes again.

It was so easy to get distracted by her. It was so easy to forget that she might actually be the person to inherit Annick Castle.

Why couldn't he have met her in a bar? Why couldn't he have just met her in the street?

Anywhere but here. And any set of circumstances but these.

Callan was usually good with people. He could usually tell the charlatans at fifty paces.

And there was definitely more to Laurie than met the eye.

But could it all just be a game?

He had to remember she could inherit this place. He had to push aside the way his pulse quickened when she entered a room, and raced when she shot him one of her winning smiles.

She was a lawyer. She was on the ball. And despite how uninterested she acted, she'd probably checked out all the legal implications before she got here. Was there a chance she was playing him?

A horrible sensation crept over his skin. Who better to tell her everything she'd need to know about Annick Castle than him? There was no one. No one else.

He'd noticed her talking to Frank Dalglish yesterday when she'd arrived, but Frank wasn't giving anything away. He was much too cautious for that.

And she'd just told him she already knew who the murderer was. At the end of the day that was all that was needed to inherit Annick Castle. He had no idea what would happen if more than one person got it right. Doubtless, Frank would have instructions for that scenario too.

He'd thought Laurie was genuinely interested in the place and the people. But maybe she was just killing time? Come Monday and the announcement of who would inherit, a totally new Laurie Jenkins might appear.

'Callan?' Laurie was tugging his arm now, concern written all over her face. 'What's wrong?' she hissed.

Robin was finishing a long diatribe at the end of the table. It seemed everyone had been listening but him. Some people were even taking notes. Had he given away a clue as to who the murderer was—or wasn't?

Truth was he didn't have a clue. About anything.

'Tomorrow night, more will be revealed as Annick Castle hosts its very own ball.' Robin's normally high-pitched voice was practically squeaking with excitement. 'Formal dress will be required—all available from our costume room, of course. I look forward to seeing you all there.'

Laurie gasped and put her hand up to her mouth. He could almost see all her childhood fantasies dancing about in her head.

Callan pushed his chair out and stood up. 'Sorry, Laurie, something's come up. We'll talk later.' He couldn't stand it. He couldn't stand the thought of all this merriment in Annick Castle.

Not when Angus McLean wasn't here to see it.

None of this seemed right. None of it at all.

# CHAPTER SEVEN

THIS WAS, WITHOUT doubt, Laurie's favourite room in the whole castle.

She leaned back in the well-worn leather chair and turned the pages of the book in front of her. It was one of the classics—*Anne of Green Gables*—and she'd never had the chance to read it before.

Her feet were tucked under her and the sun was streaming through the multi-paned windows. She took a deep breath. She loved that. The inhalation of the smell of books and wood.

The library was one of the grandest rooms in the castle. Set in the base of one of the large drum towers, the circular bookshelves ran along the inside of the room on three different levels. There was even a sliding set of stairs that allowed you to reach the books on the top level. But the real pièce de résistance was the views all around the tower. Sitting in the middle of the room Laurie could see the sea on one side and the beautiful gardens on the other. The room was every book lover's dream.

The knock at the door startled her. She'd closed the door and turned the key in the lock in order to try and have a little privacy. Just her, the views, the books and a steaming-hot cup of lemon tea.

She shrank down into the chair. It was silly. No one could see through the door. No one could really know she was in here. Maybe if she just kept quiet they would go away?

But no. The knock was more insistent this time, sharper and louder. She cringed.

'Laurie? Laurie, I know you're in there. Can you open the door, please?'

She straightened in her chair. Callan.

After his abrupt departure last night she hadn't seen him again.

She had no idea what she'd said or done to upset him. One minute they'd been almost flirting, the next second he'd disappeared. She'd made excuses as soon as she could and tiptoed up the stairs to bed. She hadn't really been in the mood for socialising after that, her excitement about the ball all but crushed.

The knock came again. 'Laurie? Will you let me in, please?'

She sighed. Callan. This was his home. She couldn't really keep him locked out. He probably had a master key somewhere anyway.

She walked over and opened the door, not even waiting to speak to him but crossing back to her chair, sitting down and picking her book back up.

He was carrying a tray in his hands that he set down on one of the tables before turning and locking the door again.

The fresh smell of his aftershave drifted across the room. She was trying to make a point by ignoring him.

But ignoring a six-foot-four man who'd just locked them both in a room was kind of hard.

That and the smell of bacon rolls that was floating across the room towards her.

Her stomach betrayed her and rumbled loudly. A plate landed on her lap. 'Can I interest you in some breakfast?'

She looked up. 'Is this an apology?'

He hesitated. 'It's a peace offering.'

'Did you bring ketchup?'

He lifted the bottle and shook it.

She held out her hand. 'Let me think about it while I'm eating.'

He sat down in the chair next to her with his own bacon roll and a cup of tea.

He smiled. 'I see you went for the old lock-the-door-and-keep-them-out trick.'

She was mid-chew. 'Sometimes it feels as if there are just too many people about. I mean, I know it's a big place—it's a castle, for goodness' sake. And I can always lock myself away in my room. But it's weird—sometimes I feel I just need a little space. A little time out.'

He nodded. 'I get it. I do. And I get agitated every time I see a measuring tape.'

She burst out laughing. 'I know. They were doing it again last night as I was going to bed. What is the obsession with that and taking pictures with their phone?'

He shook his head. 'I'm trying hard not to think about it. I'm sure if I go online I'll probably see half the furniture and antiques in this castle listed for sale.'

She was horrified. 'Callan? Do you really think that?'

He shrugged his shoulders. 'What other reason is there? I take it they're sending the pictures to someone to get things valued first.'

She shook her head. 'That's horrible.'

'That's life.'

He said the words so simply. As if he was finally trying to accept the fact that in the next few days Annick Castle would have a new owner. She couldn't imagine how he must be feeling. If people came into her home and started doing things like that—well, she couldn't be held responsible for her actions.

Their eyes met and there it was again. That connection she felt every time she was around him. Her breath hitched in her throat. She didn't want to drag her eyes away from his. What she really wanted was to get to the bottom of what was happening here.

They hadn't discussed it. They hadn't acknowledged it. Surely this wasn't just in her head?

Callan looked away and she took a steadying breath, bringing herself back to reality. She had to think about normal things. Things that weren't Callan McGregor.

Focus. She took a sip of her tea and looked around the room. That bacon roll had really hit the mark. 'I still don't get it. How did Angus McLean manage to have so many children that no one knew about?' She stood up and started walking around the room.

There were a few pictures of Angus in here. One with him in his army uniform in World War II. Another with him looking a little older and standing in front of the sign for Ellis Island in New York.

Callan walked over next to her. 'I've been trying to figure it out—believe me.' He pointed to the picture of Angus in his uniform. 'I've worked out that Angus was stationed in a few places throughout World War II. He was down in England for a time, then over in Canada just after the war. I think that accounts for two—or maybe even three of his children.'

'What about this one—the New York picture?'

He nodded. 'He was apparently sent there after the war to negotiate deals for the pharmaceutical company.' He raised his eyebrows. 'That would be another child.'

'Wow. The guy certainly got about.' She wrinkled her nose. 'What about my Irish relatives, then? Did he go to Ireland?'

Callan shook his head. 'I don't think so. But Mary said her mother was originally from Scotland and moved over to Ireland as a young woman.'

'A young woman with a baby on board?'

Callan shrugged. 'It's just as much a mystery to me as it is to you, Laurie.'

She couldn't help it. Talking about Angus McLean just made her frustrated. 'But how? How could he have six children and not bother with them?'

Callan slumped down into the chaise longue and put his head in his hands. She was staring out at the gardens thinking what a beautiful environment this would have been to be raised as a child. 'I've got some boxes of paperwork—old things, to go through. Maybe I'll find something there that will shed some light on all of this.'

'Should you be doing that?' Her lawyer head was instantly slotting into place. Callan wasn't related to Angus.

He looked up at her. His brow was wrinkled again and the green of his eyes seemed to make her want to step closer. He ran his fingers through his dark hair. 'That's just it, Laurie. I might not be family, but I was named as Angus's next of kin. So, until all this is sorted, I'm pretty sure I'm allowed to sort things out. At least that's what Frank tells me.'

'Wow.' She sat down next to him and automatically put her hand on his leg. It was meant to be friendly. It was meant to be reassuring—or supportive. But it was none of those things.

It was her fine fingers feeling his thick, muscular thighs. How did a guy with a desk job get thighs like that? And what did they look like when he wasn't fully dressed?

The wayward thoughts made her blush and her instant reaction was to pull her hand away. But

Callan stopped that. He put his hand over hers and gave it a squeeze.

She could swear that right now a thousand butterflies were fluttering over the skin on her hand. She couldn't stop staring at him. Even though she wanted to.

She must look like some star-struck teenager, hardly appealing.

'Didn't you know he'd named you as his next of kin?' Great. Her voice had turned into an unintelligible squeak.

He shook his head. 'Maybe I should have guessed. As far as I knew, Angus didn't really have anyone else to name as next of kin. But we'd never talked about it. I found out as he became really unwell. Frank told me.'

'But he didn't tell you the rest?'

Callan raised his eyebrows. 'That he had six mystery children? Oh, no. Frank didn't mention that.'

'Have you asked him about it?'

'That's just it. I'm not entirely sure how much Frank knows. He said he's checked back and Angus's family have dealt with Ferguson and Dalglish solicitors for years. As far as he can see, Angus was contacted at various points in his life and made payments.'

'What kind of payments?'

'I guess it must have been some sort of child support. All of this happened before I was even born.'

Laurie shook her head. 'Isn't there anyone else you can ask?'

He lifted one hand and held it up. 'Like who? Angus was ninety-seven. All his friends and acquaintances are long since gone.'

It made sense. Whether she liked it or not.

But here was the thing. She wasn't really concentrating on why Angus McLean had only acknowledged his children financially. She was far too interested in the fact that their fingers were still intertwined on his thigh. Her ability to concentrate on anything else was fading fast.

Laurie pointed at one of the photos. Anything to try and keep herself distracted. 'I have to say, I can't really see any family resemblance between Angus and my dad. I can definitely see a resemblance with some of the other relatives. I notice lots of subtle similarities between Mary from Ireland and my dad. They're half-siblings. It's only natural. But it just feels really strange. It's almost like having a little part of him back.'

Her eyes instantly filled with tears. She hadn't meant to say that out loud. She didn't want to get emotional in front of Callan.

But Callan didn't hesitate. He stood up in front of her and pulled her up, enveloping her in his arms.

She'd never been the kind of girl to act like a shrinking violet. She'd never been the kind of girl that needed rescuing by some dashing guy.

But just that act of kindness—that feeling of someone putting their arms around her—made her breath hitch in her throat. How long had it been since this had happened?

It was so nice to feel the warmth of someone's body next to hers. It was so nice to be comforted—to not feel alone any more—that for a few seconds she went with her natural responses and just buried her head against his chest. She could hear his heart thudding in her ear through the thin cotton of his shirt. She could feel the rise and fall of his chest next to her skin.

It was warm. It was comforting. It was something else entirely.

What would it be like if this could be the sound she woke up to every morning?

Her brain was doing crazy things to her today. If he'd hovered around the edges of her dream the night before, then there was no denying that he'd had the starring role last night. It was funny the things an unexpected kiss could cause to pop up in a dream.

He pulled back a little. 'Are you okay?' Before she had a chance to speak, his hand came down and tilted her chin up towards him. 'I'm sorry, Laurie. I don't mean to be a bear. I've been so caught up in the fact that Annick Castle will soon be gone that I've not really thought about how all this might be affecting others—affecting you.'

There was real sincerity in his words, real concern in his eyes. She should feel comforted. She should feel reassured. But all she could feel was the blood currently buzzing around her body.

'Angus's funeral was only a month ago. And

all this has come as a bolt out of the blue. I still wake up in the morning and it takes me a few seconds to remember that he's not here any more. It takes me a few seconds to realise I'm in the middle of all this. I feel as if I haven't really had a chance to say goodbye to him yet.'

His words stopped her blood buzzing. Stopped it dead.

She could relate. She could totally relate. Grieving was a completely individual process, but Callan's sounded similar to how she'd felt.

This time she reached out to him. And it was the most natural thing in the world for her. Her hand reached up and cradled the side of his cheek.

'I hated that. That few perfect seconds where everything was all right—just as you woke up. Then, that horrible sicky feeling you got as soon as you remembered. It was like that when my dad died. It took months for it to go away, Callan— and even now, ten years later, tiny little things— a headline in a paper, a picture of something, or someone saying something totally random to me—can bring it all flooding back. It doesn't go away. It never goes away.'

He hadn't moved. He was just watching her with his steady green eyes. He probably didn't realise it, but she could see the myriad emotions flitting behind his eyes.

She was starting to see a clearer picture now. She'd been making assumptions. But it was clear to her now that, in Callan's head, Angus had been his father figure. The person he'd relied on, the person he'd looked up to. How would she feel if she were in his shoes?

His arms were still around her waist. Her hand was still on his cheek. She almost felt frozen in time. She could stay like this for ever.

For the first time, in a long time, she felt as if she was home. Home in Callan McGregor's arms. The realisation was startling. It didn't matter how she felt about Angus McLean. She had to respect the fact that, for Callan, he'd been family.

'What happened to your own mum and dad, Callan?'

It was an intrusive question and she felt him bristle under her touch. But it was just the two of them, with no interruptions. If she wanted to understand Callan McGregor better, she had to ask.

His eyes fixed on hers and she could almost see his mind jumble around trying to decide what to say. 'My mother was never really around. I'm not entirely sure what happened in their marriage. It was only me and my dad since I was a young boy. My dad would never talk about her.'

'Do you remember anything about her?'

'I remember the police coming to the door of our house when I was fifteen to tell my dad she was dead. I was more or less staying with Angus all the time by then, but I went home on occasion.'

'What happened to her?'

He shook his head. 'I didn't actually find out until years later. She had a mental health condition—schizophrenia. She'd taken an accidental overdose.'

'That's awful. Do you think she left because of her mental health problem?'

'No. I think she left because of my dad.'

His answer was instant. The next question was poised on her lips, but something told her not to ask it. Not to pry. Callan took several deep breaths. Even sharing that little part of himself had been hard for him.

He pulled back and she was surprised by how hurt she felt as he walked across the room, picking up the plates and cups and putting them on the tray.

She didn't want him to leave. She wanted him to stay here, with her. And that made her insides curl up in confusion.

'I'll take these back to the kitchen. Are you baking today?'

The conversation was clearly over. At least that part of it was.

She took a deep breath and smiled. 'I think Marion has me lined up to make a raspberry cheesecake and some more gingerbread.'

'You could leave the staff to it, you know.'

'No. I couldn't. I like being in the kitchen. Next to this room—' she held out her arms '—it's the place I feel most at home.'

She hadn't meant to say it like that. She hadn't meant to imply that she was thinking of this place as home. Because she wasn't. Really she wasn't. Her mind was getting jumbled with the huge range of emotions Annick Castle was conjuring up for her. And something flickered across his face. A look of discomfort, that was quickly re-placed by a quick nod of the head.

'I'm going to go for another walk later—back around the grounds. Or, do you want me to help you with Angus's boxes?' It was a measured question. It was her trying to offer a hand of friendship.

Was she really comfortable making that offer? Who was she to go through Angus's things? Grandfather or not, she hadn't known him and never would. Not the way Callan had.

But she'd seen the look in Callan's eyes earlier. She'd seen how hurt he was, how he was strug-gling with his bereavement. And while she didn't have any loyalty to Angus, she did have a burn-ing desire to support Callan.

She'd been there. She knew how hard this was. Her mother had fallen to pieces and if it hadn't been for her university friends, she would have too. Having people around to support you made all the difference.

Callan shook his head. 'I'll be fine. I probably won't get much done today. I have to make some calls and answer some emails for the day job.'

She smiled. 'You mean you need to Blether?'

He laughed. 'Absolutely. I need to Blether.'

She took a deep breath. This was difficult. She was struggling with this. She didn't really know who Callan McGregor was. But he'd shared a little of himself with her today. He'd held her at the bottom of the cliff steps. He'd kissed her last night. He'd hugged her today. This was the closest she'd got to a man in months. And he set every nerve in her body on fire. There was something between them. For her, there were blurred lines all over the place. She just wasn't sure what this was.

'Well, you know where I'll be if you're looking for me.' Her eyes fixed on his.

And he held her gaze. For longer than ever before. She could practically hear the air in the room sizzle between them. Was something else going to happen?

He tore his gaze away and fixed a smile on his face. 'Yes, I do. Thanks, Laurie.' Then he picked up the tray and disappeared down the corridor.

She didn't know whether to laugh or cry.

\* \* \*

At first glance the kitchen seemed empty and Laurie walked across the room and started washing her hands at one of the Belfast sinks. It only took her a few minutes to collect all the ingredients from the larder, including the fresh raspberries that had been picked from the castle gardens this morning. She breathed in deeply; they smelled gorgeous.

She lifted the large glass mixing bowl and whisk out from the cupboard at her feet and started adding her ingredients for the cheesecake. Marion appeared at her elbow. 'Hi, Laurie, are you sure you're still happy to help?'

She jumped about a foot in the air. 'Where on earth did you come from, Marion? I was sure there was no one else in here.'

Marion laughed and tapped the side of her nose. 'I'm like the genie in the lamp. I know all the hiding places around this kitchen.'

Laurie stared at her for a few seconds, trying to work out if she was joking or not.

Marion smiled. 'I was in the pantry. You were so deep in concentration that you didn't notice me when I came out. What are you fretting about? Is it about the castle?'

Laurie set down the wooden spoon she held in her hand. 'No. It's not about the castle. Not at all.' She looked around her. 'But that's probably what I should be worrying about, isn't it?'

'Aha.'

'Aha? What does that mean?' Marion was giving her a strange kind of smile as she started to collect her own set of ingredients.

'It means I always know what's going on in this place.'

'Well, I don't. Why don't you share it with me?'

Marion was practically chuckling. 'I bet it was Callan that was on your mind.'

Her cheeks flushed instantly. The woman was a mind reader. 'Why do you think that?' Had people noticed they'd been spending time together?

'Because I've been here a long time. I notice things. I particularly notice things when it comes to Callan.' Her voice had a little protective edge to it. 'I heard about the kiss,' she added.

'How long have you been here, Marion?' Curiosity was piquing her interest, particularly now Callan had revealed a little part of himself to her.

'More than forty years.' She said the figure with pride.

'And you haven't thought about retiring?' She knew instantly it had been the wrong thing to say as Marion bristled.

'I have no intention of retiring,' she said stiffly. 'As long as I can still do my job I'll be here.'

'Of course. I didn't mean anything by it, Marion. Forty years is a long time.' She started mixing the ingredients in her bowl. 'You must have been here when Callan first appeared,' she added carefully.

Marion's keen eyes locked with hers. 'What did he tell you?'

'He told me Angus found him as a young boy. He told me about his mother. And about the fact Angus named him as next of kin.'

Marion raised her eyebrows. 'He told you quite a lot, didn't he?' Her eyes swept up and down the length of Laurie. 'He doesn't usually share much about himself.' She stopped, then added,

'But then he doesn't usually kiss girls in front of a room full of strangers.'

Laurie gave a little smile. 'I get that.'

She mixed slowly. Had she been misleading about how much Callan had told her? She was itching to know more, but she didn't want to come right out and ask.

After a few guarded seconds Marion started to speak, her eyes fixed on the wall. She'd obviously drifted off into some past memory. 'I'll never forget that night for as long as I live. When Angus came in here with Callan bundled up in his arms, freezing and soaking wet after hiding from his brute of a father.' She shook her head. 'We made a pact.'

Laurie felt her heart start to race. Did she really want to know this? Should she be upfront and tell her Callan hadn't told her this part? But the truth was she did want to know this. She wanted to understand why Callan was so fiercely loyal to Angus. She wanted to try and understand the connection between the two men.

'All of us. Me, Angus and Bert. We were the only three here that late at night. But we promised there would always be a place here for Callan. There would always be somewhere safe he could come where people would be concerned about him.' Her voice drifted off a little, and Laurie could see the tears forming in her eyes. 'Where people could show him that they cared what happened to him.'

She looked out of the window. 'Social services weren't the same as they are nowadays. Children were left in conditions they shouldn't be. Everyone knew that.' She turned to face Laurie. 'Do you know after his drunken rage his father didn't even know that Callan had gone? It was two days before he turned up here looking for him.' Laurie could hear the disgust in her voice. 'We all knew that his mother was gone. But no one really knew why. We didn't know about the schizophrenia then.' She waved her hand. 'That all came much later.' She shook her head. 'We guess that his father got worse after his mother left. But we don't know that for sure. Maybe his father's drinking contributed towards his mother's mental health condition? All I know is, that must have been a terrible environment for a wee boy to be in.'

Laurie was shocked. No wonder Callan only shared little pieces of himself. What had he been subjected to at home?

Marion hadn't said the words but the implication about his father being a drunk was clear. She couldn't help the automatic shiver that ran down her spine. No child should be subjected to a life like that.

Her eyes fixed on the contents of the bowl as she stirred. She could feel the tears prickling in her eyes. Her natural thoughts were to compare Callan's upbringing with her own.

She'd had a mum and dad who had loved her dearly and doted on her. Callan's life had been nothing like that. And no matter what her thoughts about Angus McLean, thank goodness he'd recognised a child in need and had reached out to him.

She felt a hand resting on her back. Marion's. 'I know,' came the quiet words of understanding. Marion could obviously see the whole host of emotions flitting across her face.

She waited a few minutes, lost in her thoughts. 'Marion, if you've been here that long, tell me about my grandfather. Tell me why he didn't acknowledge his children.'

She couldn't stop this. It played on her mind constantly. She already knew Callan's thoughts on all of this. Maybe Marion could offer better insight?

Marion shrugged her shoulders. 'I'm not sure, Laurie. It seems odd. But Angus McLean's life wasn't entirely easy. He was much more involved in the pharmaceutical business than his colleagues thought. He would spend hours in the laboratories. He was involved in all the developmental work. Lots of people just thought Angus dealt only with contracts and sales—but that wasn't true at all.'

There was something strange about her words. Something Laurie couldn't quite put her finger on.

'But lots of people have difficult jobs, Marion. That doesn't stop them keeping in contact with their kids.'

Marion's lips pressed firmly together. 'Things

aren't always what they seem, Laurie. And re-member, times have changed rapidly over the last few years. Angus did what he thought was right for his children.'

Money. Marion was talking about money. So, she wasn't wrong about this vibe. There was def-initely something that Marion wasn't telling her.

'All the money in the world doesn't make up for not having your dad when you need him, Mar-ion. I can't imagine not having my dad there. I'm a grown adult now, and I still struggle with the fact I can't pick up the phone and speak to him every day.'

'I understand that, Laurie, really I do. But ev-eryone's life circumstances are different. That's all I'm saying.' She picked up the mixture she'd been preparing and started dividing it into tins. It was clear that from her perspective the con-versation was over.

Laurie followed suit. It only took a few min-utes to finish whisking the cheesecake and put it in the fridge to set. The gingerbreads were ready for the oven and now all she had to do was wait.

'Have you finished up?'

She nodded. 'Is there something else you need a hand with?'

Marion shook her head. 'We're all ready for the ball tonight. The turkey and the beef joints are in the oven. The veg are all prepared. And I've got a few girls coming in from the village to help serve again.'

'What else is happening tonight?'

Marion rolled her eyes. 'I have no idea. I do know that there's a string quartet coming. They are expected to arrive in the next few hours. As for the rest of Robin's plans? Your guess is as good as mine.' She brushed her hands together and glanced over at the ovens. 'If you're finished up I'll be happy to take everything out of the oven for you.'

Laurie smiled. 'Has Callan been nagging you about me being in the kitchen?'

Marion laughed. 'Don't you worry about Callan nagging me. I've been dealing with that for years.'

Laurie took off her apron and hung it back up. 'I'd quite like to go for a walk around the grounds before tonight—you know, to clear my head.'

Marion nodded and looked at her carefully. 'We all need to do that sometimes. Even Callan.'

Her feet had already carried her to the door but she turned as Marion spoke again. 'Laurie—just so you know. That's the first time I've ever known Callan to be so...' she was obviously searching for the right word '...affectionate in public.'

Laurie's heart gave a little leap. She gave Marion a little smile and fled out of the door. Annick Castle was going to land her in a whole heap of trouble.

# CHAPTER EIGHT

CALLAN CHECKED THE records one more time. Annick Castle was in trouble. Lots of trouble. It was losing money like a leaky sieve. In a few weeks' time he and Frank would have to hand over all this information to the new owner. What would they think? Because right now, all paths seemed to lead to the fact that Angus McLean hadn't been managing at all.

He could see what the problems were. The biggest, and most obvious, was that Annick Castle had no income. The gas and electricity bills had quadrupled in the last ten years, but, then again, so had every family's in the country.

Annick Castle wasn't environmentally friendly. It was a draughty old girl, in rapid need of some maintenance. But even then his hands were tied. There were no modern windows to keep the freezing winter temperatures out, no proper insulation, no modern heating or modern appliances. The whole place really needed to be rewired. But rewiring was more than a little expensive, and the damage that would be incurred rewiring a building like this would be astronomical. The heritage people would have a fit. As for the roof…

He hadn't even had a chance to glance at Angus's boxes yet. All his time had been taken up with trying to sort out the accounts. It wasn't just the castle. The family fortune had been damaged by the stock-market crash, some unlucky investments and poor interest rates. He was going to have to try and find some solutions—fast.

He closed the computer program and grabbed his jacket. The walls were starting to close in around him. He needed some fresh air and that was one thing Annick Castle had in abundance. It was time to find Laurie. She was the only person around here he wanted to spend any time with.

Part of him felt a little guilty that he didn't want to spend more time around Angus's children or grandchildren. Truth was, some of them he didn't even like.

And a tiny part of him said why should he

spend time with people that Angus hadn't? And until he got to the bottom of that he wouldn't be able to understand it.

But Laurie was different. She wasn't constantly assessing the value of the castle. She wasn't aligning herself with estate agents as he'd heard one of Angus's sons doing yesterday.

Laurie was the only one of Angus's relatives he felt a connection to. He couldn't understand it. He couldn't understand it at all, but after several hours surrounded by computers, paperwork and figures he found himself craving her company again.

It would be so much easier if he could put Laurie Jenkins in a box where she wasn't a possible inheritor of the castle, and she wasn't Angus McLean's granddaughter. Then maybe he would be free to try and figure out what it was about her that drew him like a moth to a flame.

The scent of gingerbread had drawn him to the kitchen. But the evidence of her baking was sitting on two wire cooling trays with no sign of Laurie at all.

He walked out into the grounds. His first guess

had been the gazebo next to the swan pond. He'd noticed the gleam in her eyes when she'd first seen it and the whole host of other thoughts that was obviously flitting around her mind. But even from the top of the steps leading to the lowered gardens it was clear she was nowhere in sight.

His steps carried him onwards, quickening as his brain went into overdrive. *Please don't let her have headed to the caves.* It was odd. He hadn't given a second thought to any of the other relatives injuring themselves on the cliff-side stairs—even though they would probably sue Annick Castle—his only thought was for Laurie. The thought of her on those stairs sent a shudder down his spine. He really needed to see about something more substantial than a piece of rope to block them off.

He rounded the drum tower and stopped dead.

There she was. A yellow hard hat perched precariously on her head as she skirted around the edges of the round icehouse. She hesitated at the entrance, glancing at the roof, then in the blink of an eye she disappeared inside.

He resisted the temptation to shout at her, striding over and grabbing one of the other hard hats outside and jamming it on his head. He'd warned her about this place. It wasn't safe. Part of the roof had already fallen in, and other parts looked distinctly dangerous.

He stuck his head inside. It was much darker in here. The only window was boarded up and there was no lighting, no electricity. The place hadn't been used in over one hundred years.

'Laurie? What are you doing?'

She was standing in the middle of the icehouse, looking up at the part of the ceiling that had fallen in. Could she be any more dangerous?

'I just wanted to get a feel for the place, Callan. You talked about the history of the caves, but what about the history of this place?'

He folded his arms across his chest. 'It was an icehouse. It stored ice that was brought up from the lake. It took the ice to the kitchen. End of.'

She walked over towards him. Even in this dim light he could see the sparkle in her eyes. Her voice changed timbre. 'Callan McGregor, are you using your stern voice on me?'

'Do I need to?' His response was instant because Laurie Jenkins had gone from the middle of the room to directly under his nose. Didn't she realise what those big brown eyes did to the men around her? Had this woman no idea of the electricity she could spark with those few words? She was flirting with him. She was definitely flirting.

'Hmm...' She was looking up at him through half-closed lids. In another life he'd have called them come-to-bed eyes. But Laurie didn't seem the type.

But type or not, her very presence was having instant effects on his body.

She gave a shiver and he frowned. 'Are you cold, Laurie?'

Why hadn't he even considered that? He'd picked her up from the railway station; he knew she'd travelled light. He was wearing a big thick parka, the one he always used for tramping around the grounds of Annick Castle. But Laurie only had on a light summer jacket. It might be nearing the end of summer, but she obviously hadn't banked on the Scottish coastal winds.

'Isn't it weird? How even though this place

hasn't been used in years, it's just still so…cold.' She gave a shudder and wrapped her arms around herself.

Callan moved closer, opening his jacket and putting one arm around her shoulders. He couldn't quite fit her inside, but she slid her arm behind his waist and pressed her body up next to his.

He tried to focus. 'What are you doing in here anyway?'

She smiled. 'It's this place. I like it. I love the shape—the circular building is gorgeous. And it's bigger than you'd expect. Why didn't Angus do something with this? Turn it into something else?'

Callan shook his head. 'Like what? He's already got two unused sets of stables, a gazebo, an orangery, an old water house, an old gas house, and—' he gestured out beyond the doors '—a whole set of mystery caves.'

But Laurie was deep in thought, her mind obviously taking her off into her own world. 'This could be a gorgeous coffee shop,' she murmured, 'right next to the castle, with views over the sea and over the gardens if this place had windows in it. It could make a fortune.'

The words sent prickles over his skin. Did Laurie know more about Annick Castle than she was letting on?

But she was obviously wrapped up in her own ideas. 'Can't you see it, Callan?' She held her arms out. 'Just think, wooden tables and chairs with red and white checked tablecloths. A whole variety of teas.' She pointed to the other side of the round house. 'There could be a whole circular serving area over here and one of those gorgeous coffee machines.' Her eyes were lit up. 'I can practically smell the different kinds of scones, gingerbread, sponges and chocolate buns. You could serve local produce from the neighbouring farms, maybe even from the castle gardens?' She was walking around, obviously seeing the whole thing in her head. 'It could be great. Two kinds of homemade soup every day and a different variety of scone.' She came back over and slid her arm around his waist again.

He could feel himself bristle. 'What's the point?

The castle isn't open to the public. Who would come to a coffee shop?'

'But maybe it should be.' Her eyes looked up and met his.

He drew in a sharp breath. Her words put him instantly on the defensive.

And Laurie seemed to sense that, but she waved her hand. 'Oh, don't get all crabbit with me, Callan. I'll be the first person to admit I know nothing about Annick Castle. But I'm not blind. I can see buildings lying in ruins. I can see the tiles and slates off the roof. That can't be safe. That can't be good for the castle. Don't you want to see things restored? Wouldn't you like it if that gorgeous pagoda that used to house birds down at the swan pond could be rebuilt? You already told me the upper floor used to be a teahouse. It seems like somebody, somewhere, at one time thought it was a good idea.'

He tried not to be defensive. He tried not to take it as a criticism. But the thought of a whole bunch of strangers tramping around Annick Castle didn't fill him with joy.

He had to be rational about this. He had to put

his business head on and think with his head and not his heart. 'Do you think people would want to come and see around Annick Castle?' There were a hundred little thoughts currently sparking around his brain. He'd only ever thought of Annick Castle as a home. He'd never even considered anything else. And deep down he knew Angus wouldn't approve of having strangers on his property. But the sad fact was that times had changed, the comfortable nest egg the family used to have was gone, and so was Angus. It was certainly something that the new owner could look into.

'Why ever not? There's another castle about a hundred miles down the coast that's open to the public. They have a kids' playground, a teahouse, an old bookshop and stables too. Why couldn't Annick Castle be like that?'

He could feel the hackles go up on the back of his neck, instantly suspicious of her wider knowledge. 'How do you know that?' His voice was low. It was practically a growl. But Callan McGregor couldn't hide how he felt about things.

Had she been planning this all along? He hated feeling as if he'd been duped.

Her arm slid out from around his waist. She folded her arms and stood in front of him. All of a sudden the dim light in the icehouse didn't seem tranquil or romantic, it felt oppressive.

'I know because I looked it up on the Internet, Callan. What did you think? That I'd planned all this before I got here?'

The words stuck in his throat. He was being ridiculous. He *knew* he was being ridiculous. He just couldn't help it. As soon as anyone started making suggestions about Annick Castle he could virtually feel his own portcullis slide down in front of him.

The protection of Annick Castle lay at the very essence of his heart and soul. He couldn't see past it. He couldn't see around it.

And being around Laurie just seemed to heighten every emotion that he felt. Magnify it ten times over. He seemed to seesaw between high as a kite and lower than the belly of a snake all in the blink of an eye.

Laurie was annoyed. It was practically emanating from her pores. And boy was she beautiful when she was angry. Her dark eyes flashed, 'Get over yourself, Callan. I *get* that you love this place. I *get* that it means everything to you. But if you find yourself unable to have a rational, reasonable conversation about the place then I've got to ask the question if you're the right person to be custodian of this place in the first place. I'm making one tiny suggestion.' She held up her finger and thumb with the minimum of space between them. 'That's all. The very least you can do is listen.'

'It's not one tiny suggestion, Laurie.' He held up his finger and thumb too, but then he held his arms open wide. 'This is the kind of suggestion you're making. Annick Castle hasn't been open to the public since its first building was put up in the fifteen-hundreds. That's more than five hundred years of history.'

She stepped closer, gritting her teeth. 'Exactly. Five hundred years of history that should be shared with others.'

Their faces were inches apart. Even in this dim light he could see the normally hidden tiny freckles that were scattered across her nose. He didn't even want to start thinking about those brown eyes again. In years gone by Laurie Jenkins would probably have been labelled an enchantress with eyes like those.

And she was obviously determined to get her point across. 'Don't you think visitors would love to know about the links with Mary Queen of Scots? Don't you think there must be dozens of little boys who'd want to explore the smuggler's caves and think about pirates? Don't you think there must be a hundred crazy women like me who'd love a chance to sit in the gazebo that matches the one in *The Sound of Music* and dream their afternoon away?'

He could see the passion in her eyes. Passion in them for Annick Castle and what it represented and he couldn't help but smile.

'You've really got it bad for that gazebo, haven't you?'

His words broke the tension in the air between them in an instant.

Her face broke into a smile too and she rolled

her eyes. 'You have *no* idea how much I love that gazebo.'

'Every little girl's dream?'

'Oh, *way* more than that.'

'Better than the castle double staircase?'

She grinned. 'Yip. Even better than the castle staircase.' She moved back towards him. 'Why is it that we always head towards a fight? What is it I do that upsets you so much?'

'I keep asking myself the same question.' His voice had deepened; it was quieter—a virtual whisper. The words seemed to echo around the circular building.

She edged a little closer and he found himself doing the same thing. Any second now he could reach out and touch her. Touch the soft skin of her face, run his fingers through her loose curls. Or just grab her with both hands and pull her body next to his.

Her sultry perfume was winding its way around him again—like the Pied Piper's music had lured the children of Hamelin. He couldn't control it.

He couldn't help the grin spreading across his face.

She blinked, her long dark eyelashes brushing against his lowered head. It was torture. 'And have you found the answer yet, Callan?'

Even the way she said his name sent shivers down his spine. His hands reached up and cradled her hips. 'It's as much a mystery to me as it is to you. Maybe we're just two people with a lot at stake.'

She squeezed her eyes shut. 'Not the answer I was looking for.'

It wasn't the answer he'd wanted to say either. But he couldn't articulate what he really wanted to say. He couldn't sort it out in his head. And until he did that, how could he say anything?

He couldn't tell her that she was driving him crazy. He couldn't tell her that he hadn't been able to sleep since he'd kissed her. He *definitely* couldn't tell her what she'd been doing in the five minutes' worth of dreams he'd had last night.

And no matter how much his body was reacting around Laurie, no matter how much he felt drawn to her. No matter how much he was attracted to her both physically and emotionally, he still had the tiniest doubts in his head. Doubts placed there by his love of Annick Castle. And until that was resolved he couldn't feel free to make any kind of other decision.

'It's the best I can do right now.'

She stepped backwards and gave him a gentle smile. 'I know, Callan, I'm finding this just as hard as you are. You aren't the only person with something at stake.'

She gave him a wink, but it wasn't the playful kind of wink he'd experienced from Laurie before. This was different. It was more resigned. Almost sad.

She looked out of the doors, her eyes drifting over towards the crashing waves. 'There's something about this place, Callan. I can't tell you what it is. I can't put my finger on it. But Annick Castle, it just draws you in and holds you here.'

He understood. He understood completely. He always had, right from the first time he'd stayed here. Was it the dream of living in a castle, or was it just the austerity of the building, the magic of the surroundings?

And this was it. This was the tiny thing that kept creeping up on him. It was the long tendrils

of jealousy that flickered around him when someone else said those words. When Annick Castle
had that effect on *them*.

Her words tailed off. 'But is it the castle...' then
her dark eyes fixed on his again and a jolt shot
through him '...or is it you?'

She disappeared out of the door before he could
reply.

His skin prickled. It didn't matter what his self-
ish thoughts were. Laurie Jenkins had just laid
it on the line.

Big time.

She'd only lain down on the bed for a few minutes. But it seemed as if the comfortable mattress
and high thread-count sheets had lulled her off
into a deep sleep. As her eyes flickered open the
sun was lowering in the sky outside her window.
It wouldn't be sunset for a few hours yet but she'd
slept much later than she'd expected.

A wave of panic swept over her as she glanced
at her watch. She jumped from the bed and ran to
the door. The ball was tonight and she had nothing to wear. She hadn't even given it a thought;

she'd been too busy baking in the kitchen and spending time with Callan. The costume room was on the floor underneath and her feet thudded heavily down the stairs. She'd always managed to find something suitable before; she would just have to grab the first thing that fitted.

Robin was flapping around the room. Flapping. It was the most accurate expression for him. 'There you are! Where have you been? You're the only person who hasn't chosen a costume.'

'Sorry, Robin, I fell asleep. I'll just take whatever you think is appropriate.'

He pointed to the wall. 'I'd already picked out a few possibilities for you.'

There were four dresses hanging from part of the coving on the wall. Should he really be doing that? Wouldn't that damage the paintwork? She shuddered to think.

The costume room was packed full of colourful clothes, all hanging in rails by gender and size. Some women would absolutely adore this, but Laurie had never been the kind to spend hours mooning over clothes. She appreciated beautiful things, but didn't want to spend the time having to find them. The last two dresses she'd had from this room Robin had recommended to her.

She walked over to the four dresses. All beautiful. All full-length. She wasn't quite as elegant as others might think. There was a high possibility of her catching her feet in these dresses and tumbling down the curved staircase. That would make for an interesting ball.

She reached out and touched one. There was a variety of colours. Gem colours. Ruby red, emerald green, sapphire blue and silver. All sparkling. All gorgeous.

She wrapped her arms around herself and turned to face Robin.

'What's wrong?' he demanded. 'Don't you like them?'

She screwed up her face; she really didn't want to hurt his feelings. She hesitated before speaking. 'I think they're all beautiful. But I'm worried about wearing something full-length. It just isn't me. There's a strong likelihood I'll fall over and ruin them.'

He scowled and touched the red one. 'It's a ball, Laurie. You're supposed to wear something full-length—you know, a *ball* gown. I thought you might go for this one. It's almost identical to the dress the girl is wearing in the picture at the top of the stairs.'

He was getting tetchy. She looked again. It was. It was perfect. A little more old-fashioned than the others but almost a perfect replica. Why couldn't she imagine herself wearing it? It was so thoughtful that Robin had tried to take in the surroundings. But she just couldn't picture herself walking down the stairs in that dress. If there were ghosts in this castle they'd probably push her down in disgust at her attempts to look regal.

She shook her head. 'I'm sorry, Robin. I just don't think they're right for me.'

He let out a loud sigh and threw up his hands. 'Okay then, Laurie. What is it? What is the dress you see in your dreams?'

She laughed. 'It depends entirely what I'm dreaming about.'

'Pfft.' He waved his hand in disgust and touched his finger to the side of her forehead. 'What is it, Laurie? What's the one that you keep in here?' Then his finger came down and pressed on her chest bone. 'Or more importantly, what's the one you keep in here?'

She flinched. 'It's the dress Liesl wore in *The Sound of Music*.' The words came straight out without a second thought.

'No!' He was excited, and obviously a little surprised. He didn't even have to ask what dress she was referring to as he clearly already knew. He flung his arms around her. 'Oh, Laurie, you are going to love me!'

He disappeared in a flurry, snaking amongst the rails of clothing.

She caught her breath; he couldn't have what she was looking for—could he? She stood on her tiptoes. Robin had disappeared from sight. She'd no idea where he'd disappeared to, then she heard an exclamation of pure pleasure. 'I've got it!'

He snaked his way back through to her, a pale pink dress held in a plastic cover in his hands. Her heart started to beat a little faster and she was sure her eyes must have been as wide as saucers. 'No. You can't have.'

'I can.' He swept the dress past her in pleasure, holding it up under the light. 'A genuine, replica

Liesl dress.' She'd never seen him look so pleased with himself.

Laurie could hardly contain her excitement. She reached out her hands to touch the dress, then snatched them back again.

Robin lifted his eyebrows; it was almost as if he understood. He slipped the dress out of its protective cover and held the hanger in one hand and let the dress rest on his forearm.

It was the palest pink chiffon, as light as a whisper. Elbow-length chiffon sleeves, a tiny bow in the middle of the gathered bodice, and a knee-length swishy skirt. It was exactly the same as the dress in the film.

There were no sequins. No floor-length glamour. No jewels. But beauty was in the eye of the beholder and it was the most perfect dress she'd ever seen.

The colour was so pale. On so many other women the colour would completely wash them out. But Laurie had slightly sallow skin, and with her dark eyes and long brunette curls there was no doubt it would suit her to perfection.

'Will it fit me?' She was almost too scared to

ask. She had curves. She certainly wasn't the tiny frame of the actress who'd played Liesl in the film.

Robin nodded with pride. 'I promise, it will be a perfect fit.'

She held out her hands. She had to touch it and she couldn't wait to try it on.

Her feet flew up the stairs even quicker than she'd come down. She slammed the door behind her and stripped off her clothes in an instant, sliding her arms through the delicate material.

It fell over her head as light as a feather. Her eyes were closed and she spun around to where the full-length mirror was, praying inside her head that it would look okay.

She opened her eyes. It looked more than okay. It was more perfect than she could have imagined. It was almost as if it had been made especially for her.

She glanced at her watch. She'd only half an hour to get ready. She pulled the dress over her head again and switched on the shower. It only took her a few minutes to put her long hair in sticky rollers. There was a knock at the door.

She panicked and grabbed a towel to hold in front of herself in her undressed state. She opened the door just a crack. It was Robin, holding two pairs of shoes in his hands.

He rolled his eyes at her. 'You dashed off so quickly I didn't have time to give you some shoes. Take your pick.' He held up the first pair. 'Nude shoes—' then held up the other '—or gold sparkly sandals. Not strictly Liesl,' he whispered, 'but aren't they gorgeous?'

He set them on the floor just outside her door. 'I'll leave them here.' He sashayed back down the corridor as she clutched at her towel and grabbed the shoes.

She could hear the strains of music downstairs. The string quartet had obviously arrived and was setting up. Robin had also left her a card with her instructions for her character this evening. She hadn't even glanced at it and it made her feel guilty. He'd obviously just pushed the boat out to give her what she wanted. The least she could do was try and fulfil her duties for this evening.

But the shower was calling and time was ticking onwards. She didn't want to be late.

She got ready in double-quick time, pulling out her rollers at the last possible second and letting her curls tumble around her shoulders. At the last minute she fastened her gold locket around her neck, giving it a little kiss. 'You've no idea what's going on, Dad,' she whispered. 'I just hope you'd approve.'

She slipped one foot into one of the nude shoes and pulled the straps of one of the gold sandals over the other. A quick glimpse in the full-length mirror told her everything she wanted to know.

The nude shoes were abandoned and the straps on the sandals quickly fastened into place. A little brush of eye shadow and mascara and some rose-coloured lipstick and she was ready.

She read over the instructions on the card once more. She really didn't have much to do this evening. A simple conversation with one of the other guests, which would obviously lead them to think her a suspect. Robin was planting red herrings all over the place.

She didn't really care. It wasn't important. Not to her.

She wanted to enjoy herself. She wanted to

enjoy spending the evening in Annick Castle when it would look at its finest. Where she could imagine bygone eras and what the nights had been like for the people who used to be residents here.

Where she could spend some more time with Callan McGregor.

Where she could try and figure out what was going on in her head whenever she was around him.

Tiny pieces were fitting into place. Callan had opened up a little, but after Marion's telling comments she finally felt as if she could start to appreciate the loyalty he felt towards Angus McLean.

It was exactly the same as the loyalty she felt towards her father. She had one final glance out of the window towards the sea and then walked across the room, pulling the door closed behind her.

She walked along the corridor. How would she feel about going back to her flat in London? Being surrounded by the compressed air of the city again instead of the fresh coastal winds of the Scottish Highlands?

Her feet carried her along the corridor. One foot in front of the other.

*One foot in front of the other.* Much as her life had been for the last eight years. But was that enough? Didn't she want more out of life?

Her eyes had been opened in the last few days to a whole host of possibilities—both personal and professional.

How would it feel to get up every morning feeling excited about going to work? How would it feel to be doing something else entirely?

She reached the top of the curved stairways and looked down to the magnificent hallway. Which set of stairs, one or the other? And how did you choose?

She glanced at the red-dressed woman in the portrait at the top of the stairs. Her haughty expression hadn't changed. But there was more. Something else when you looked a little closer. Something in her eyes. Something pleading. Was it desperation?

There was a shift in her peripheral vision.

Callan. He was waiting at the bottom of the stairs for her. It didn't matter which set of stairs she walked down. The outcome would be the same.

It was almost as if someone had turned on a glistening chandelier in her head.

The last few days had been the oddest of her life.

Relief. That was what she'd felt as soon as she'd set foot in Annick Castle.

No tension headaches. No aching joints or sleepless nights. Her stomach coiled at the realisation that was coming over her.

She couldn't go back. She couldn't go back to Bertram and Bain. No matter what happened here.

Just the recognition in her brain felt like a huge weight off her shoulders. The logistics of how she might do that were too complicated for her to figure out herself. She had ongoing cases—responsibilities to clients. It was only fair that she work a period of notice.

The fear of stepping outside her ordered life was terrifying. She really needed to speak to someone about it. But who? Most of her friends were in the profession, and they would be horrified and try to talk her out of it.

Callan. He was the only person she could talk to about it.

He was the only person she wanted to talk to about this.

And there he was—waiting for her. Everything about this just seemed right.

She took the first step.

## CHAPTER NINE

CALLAN WAS AGITATED. He'd spent the last five minutes walking about the drawing room, dining room and kitchen. Searching everywhere for Laurie, but she wasn't here yet.

Everyone else seemed to be accounted for. Most were sipping drinks and listening to the string quartet—who were surprisingly good. Marion was a blur in the kitchen; service would begin shortly. So where was Laurie?

For a horrible fleeting second he wondered if she'd decided to leave. To get away from Annick Castle and to get away from him.

She'd left that question hanging in the air between them. She'd been disappointed he couldn't acknowledge what was happening between them. And he'd been disappointed too.

If he got her on her own again he wouldn't make the same mistake.

The momentary thought of her leaving vanished as quickly as it had come. He'd seen the look in her eyes. He'd seen the way she felt about her surroundings. Laurie wasn't ready to leave yet. No matter how many difficult conversations they had.

Then he froze. There she was. Standing at the top of the curved staircase.

Looking as if she belonged. Looking as if she was meant to be here.

She was a vision. No ball gown. Nothing ostentatious.

It took him a few seconds for the vaguely familiar-looking dress to click into place in his head. Of course. He should have known.

He watched her carefully. She was deep in thought, her hand resting on the carved banister. She was taking long slow breaths, then her eyes met his and she gave him a smile as her feet started to descend the stairway.

She was breathtakingly beautiful. Her shiny dark curls danced around her shoulders. The simple pink chiffon dress floated around her, emphasising the curves of her breasts and hips.

But it wasn't just her beauty that was captivating. It was something else. It was the feeling that she looked totally at home—that walking down this staircase was what she was supposed to be doing.

He met her at the bottom of the stairs. 'Should I break into song?' he said quietly.

He couldn't wipe the smile from her face. Her eyes sparkled and her cheeks were flushed. 'I need to talk to you. I need to tell you something.'

He frowned. 'Is something wrong?'

She shook her head, making her curls bounce around. 'No. I think for the first time in a long time, something is right.'

He had no idea what she was talking about. All he could see was how happy she looked, how relaxed. It was almost as if the weight of the world had been lifted off her shoulders. What on earth had happened?

He crooked his elbow towards her. 'Shall we go into dinner?'

She nodded and slipped her arm through his. 'I can't wait for this to be over,' she whispered in his ear.

'Me either. Do you have anything to do this evening?'

She shrugged. 'I've to have a conversation with someone and say a few things that will make them suspicious of me.'

'I've to do something similar.' They'd reached the dining room by this point and he pulled out her chair for her, ignoring the seating plan at the table. As she sat down he moved the cards around.

She arched her eyebrow at him. 'I've taught you well.'

He sat beside her. 'You have. I feel kind of guilty—I haven't really paid much attention to what's been happening this weekend.' He didn't mean for the words quite to come out like that. He'd been paying far too much attention to what was happening between them, just not the events of the Murder Mystery Weekend.

He could see her pause momentarily before she took a sip of her rosé wine. 'I haven't either,' she said, her eyes fixing on his.

For a moment he felt relief. She hadn't misunderstood. She was staring at him with those big brown eyes. He couldn't blink. He didn't want to do anything to break this moment. She knew he was invested heavily in Annick Castle. She knew how important it was to him. She knew he loved it with every breath that he took.

So, to allow himself to be distracted away from the events of the weekend spoke volumes. He was only just beginning to realise how much.

Laurie Jenkins was occupying every waking minute of his thoughts. She was burrowing under his skin with her questions, her logic and her passion for everything around her. Maybe he should be worried. Maybe, given the set of circumstances he was in, he should be acting with more caution. But Laurie was the first woman he'd ever really felt a true connection with.

Of course, he'd had girlfriends. He'd even lived with one woman for a couple of years. But he'd never felt this. He'd never felt drawn to someone so much.

And it wasn't for any of the reasons most people would suspect. It wasn't her connection to Angus—if anything, that was more of a hindrance than a help. And it wasn't the possibility she could inherit Annick Castle.

No. This was simple. This was all about her, Laurie Jenkins, and him, Callan McGregor.

He would have felt this way no matter where he'd met her. Whether it had been some noisy bar in London or Edinburgh, or some workplace environment. The fact that he'd met her here—in one of the most beautiful settings in the world—was just an added bonus.

One he fully intended to take advantage of.

He gave her a smile. There was a whole host of other thoughts going on in his head that he almost hoped she could see. 'I guess it's only good manners for us to stay as long as it takes to fulfil our duties.'

She nodded solemnly, with a wicked smile dancing across her lips. 'I guess you're right.' She leaned forward and whispered in his ear, 'How long *exactly* do you think that will take?'

Their eyes met again and stayed that way until Robin clapped his hands together to draw their attention. 'Good evening, people. This is the last night of our Murder Mystery Weekend. There have been more than enough clues left for you all to have some idea of who the murderer could be. I'd ask you *all*—' he emphasised the word and looked pointedly in the direction of Laurie and Callan '—to pay special attention to the actions you've been asked to take this evening that will help all parties have an equal chance of winning the castle.'

Callan felt a cold wave wash over his skin. Robin made it sound as if they were winning the lottery—not an ancient piece of history. He tried to push his thoughts aside. He had to come to terms with this. He had to move past this and accept Angus's decision. The boxes upstairs flickered into his mind again. He had to spend some time looking through them. Not that it would make any difference to the eventual outcome.

A slim hand slipped under the table and gave his hand a squeeze. Even now Laurie was taking his thoughts into consideration. The touch of her silky skin sent a shot of electricity up his arm, setting his senses on fire. And in a world of uncertainty there was one thing that he knew for sure. Nothing would douse these flames.

He kept his voice low. 'How quickly can you eat dinner, Laurie?'

She smiled as a bowl of soup was placed in front of her. 'Quicker than you can imagine.' She looked around her. 'This is my last night in Annick Castle. Let's blow this place as quickly as we can.'

She was laughing. She wanted to escape the confines of the dining room and their other companions and he felt exactly the same.

Dinner had never seemed such a protracted affair. The food was as delicious as always. But every single mouthful seemed to take for ever. People were too busy talking to eat their food. In between courses Callan walked around to the other side of the table and had the conversation that his card had instructed him to. It was over in the blink of an eye. He made sure of it.

And Laurie had done the same. But she didn't seem to walk—she floated. Something was different with her tonight. And he couldn't wait to find out what.

The clock ticked slowly. By the time dessert arrived Callan wanted to refuse it and leave. But it was Marion's speciality, rhubarb compote with crème anglaise and he could never offend her by not eating her food.

Laurie was more relaxed. She happily sipped her wine and ate her food, chatting to all those around her. By the time Robin announced time for coffee in the drawing room Callan was almost ready to explode.

He didn't hesitate. He grabbed her hand and pulled her towards the open glass doors leading out to the gardens. 'Ready to leave?'

She flashed him a smile. 'Around two hours ago.'

'Really? You seemed so comfortable.'

'I'm just a better actor than you.' She squeezed his hand. 'Where are we going?'

They'd walked out to the stone patio that overlooked the maze. There was smoke around them, a haze. A natural mist that was lifting from the sea as the warm summer air met the cool sea breezes. If he didn't know any better he'd suspect some film director was pumping it around them to set the scene.

But Callan didn't need anyone else to set the scene for him. He'd arranged that for himself.

He looked down at her. 'In that dress? There's only one place we can go.'

They didn't even wait to walk along the paths but just cut across the lawn towards the stairs that led to the lowered gardens. His hand was grasping hers tightly and she could scarcely keep up with his long strides, the damp grass wetting her feet through the open gold sandals. As the grass was wet the ground underneath it was soft, her spindly heels sinking rapidly into the pliable earth. She stumbled as her heel caught and her foot slipped out of the shoe.

Callan's strong arms closed around her, catching her before she collided with the damp grass. 'Careful!'

He reached back and extracted her shoe from the ground, kneeling down to slip it back over her foot. His gentle touch around her foot was sending a whole host of delicious tingles down her spine as he refastened the straps. 'Isn't this what Cinderella did? Lose her shoe as she ran away from the ball?'

She smiled at him. Her one leg that was on the ground was feeling distinctly wobbly. 'I guess that makes you my Prince Charming, then?'

His hand slid along her lower leg. The tingles were getting *so* much worse. 'I guess it does.' He stood up, stopping in front of her for a few seconds. She caught her breath.

This was so real now.

Tonight was their last night together. And expectations were causing the air between them to sizzle.

He reached out and took her hand again, this time walking with a little more care, a little more measure.

As they reached the top of the stairway she let out a little gasp. Something she totally hadn't expected. Lights around the gazebo.

'I didn't realise,' she began. 'Is there an electricity supply down there?'

The rest of the swan pond was in complete darkness. Even the steps they were standing on now had no lighting.

'No. Just be thankful for modern technology.'

She took a few tentative steps down the first few stairs and screwed up her nose. 'What is it then?'

'Solar lights. Small white ones lighting around the base of the gazebo, and some coloured butterfly lights strung along the outside.'

'They're beautiful, Callan. Just beautiful.' She tilted her head as she looked at him. 'Have they always been there? I didn't notice them the other day.'

He shook his head. 'I put them there today.'

There was a little soar of pleasure in her chest. It was almost as if, with every step, a notch on the dial between them turned up. She felt curious. 'Did you know? Did you know about the dress?'

'No. But I knew about your daydream. You told me. You told me what you wanted to do.'

Her heart squeezed in her chest. She hadn't told him everything she wanted to do. Some thoughts were entirely private. But here, and now, someone had valued her enough to make her little girl dreams come true. Someone she'd only known for a few days, but felt a whole-hearted connection to.

'Thank you,' she whispered.

He kept her hand in his as she walked gingerly down the steps and they walked along the white stone path around the edge of the swan pond. She could hear the swans rustling in the bushes at the side of the pond. Some of them were floating near to the edges, obviously asleep. It was such a peaceful setting at night.

The gazebo with its soft lights was glowing like a beacon in the middle of the pitch-black night. Twinkling like a Christmas tree in the middle of summer. The air around them was still with hardly a breath of air. Apart from the occasional animal noise all she could hear was their steps on the path, the stones crunching beneath their feet. It was magical.

They reached the entrance to the gazebo and Callan pushed the door open. It creaked loudly. Almost in protest at being disturbed. She liked the idea that none of the other guests had been here. She liked the thought that this was her and Callan's private space.

It probably wasn't too surprising. Most of the other guests were older than her and Callan. The steps to the lower garden were steep, not the most conducive to those who weren't as steady on their feet.

She held her breath as she stepped inside. Wow. The glass panels inside reflected the string of tiny butterfly lights outside. And as they bobbed around outside, the multicoloured lights reflected across the floor inside like a rainbow.

It was better than a movie effect. This was real.

She felt his hands on her waist and spun around to face him, her hands reaching up and resting on the planes of his chest.

He smiled down at her. 'So, Laurie. What is it you wanted to talk to me about?' He was standing over her. Only inches away.

She was trying to concentrate. She was trying not to focus on the rise and fall of his chest beneath the palms of her hands. She was trying not to dare recognise the fact she could feel the gentle echo of his beating heart beneath her fingertips.

It was time. It was time to tell someone else her plans. Her hopes for the future. It didn't matter that she didn't know where those plans would take her. She only knew they wouldn't keep her in London any more.

Callan's green eyes were focused on her. And they soothed her. And they ignited a fire within her belly. A surge she hadn't felt in a long time.

'You know I work as a lawyer in London.'

He nodded.

'When you told me that you worked in computers instead of mathematics I was surprised.'

'Why?' His voice was quiet. 'Lots of people do degrees in one field and take jobs in another.'

She hesitated. This was hard. She was trying so hard not to say anything she would regret. 'It's a bit more difficult when you've studied law. It's not such a generic field. Once you've done a law degree there's really only one way you can go.'

'I get it. Like why would you study medicine if you don't want to be a doctor? But why would you do a law degree if you didn't want to be a lawyer?'

It made so much more sense when he said it out loud. It also made her feel foolish. Foolish for taking so long to put this into words.

She lowered her head, blinking back the tears

that had automatically formed in her eyes. There was a lump in her throat. She felt his warm hand sweep back the hair that had covered her face, pulling it back to the nape of her neck where his gentle figures rested. 'Laurie?'

The tears started to flow. 'I knew right from the minute I got there that I didn't want to do a law degree. I'd done well at school. My guidance teacher persuaded me to apply for the best possible degrees for my results. It seemed natural. It seemed the sensible thing to do.'

'You were thinking with your head instead of your heart?'

He whispered the words as if he understood.

She nodded desperately. 'My dad—he was just so happy, so proud when he knew I'd been accepted to Cambridge. He'd never imagined his daughter would do so well. And neither did I. It all seemed like a dream at first.' She shook her head, fixating on the flickering lights outside. 'Then my dad just worked so hard, such long hours to make the dream a reality and all of a sudden I felt as if I couldn't get out. I couldn't say anything. How could I disappoint him when he was working so hard? What kind of a daughter would that make me? It was like being on a train ride I couldn't get off.'

His hand cradled the side of her cheek and his fingers brushed away one of her tears. 'You felt like you couldn't tell him?'

She nodded again as the tears just seemed to flow from her eyes like a tumbling river's stream. 'I didn't want to do anything to disappoint him. I didn't want to do anything to make him sad.' She could hear the desperation in her own voice. 'But when you said that Angus had no expectation of you beyond finishing your own degree...' Her voice tailed off. 'It just seemed unfair. You make it sound so easy.'

Her hands were resting on his shoulders now and one of his hands drifted along the length of her arm, settling back to her waist where he pulled her closer.

The temperature had dropped around them. Or maybe it was just the atmosphere that was making her breath send little clouds in the air around them. The hairs on her arms were standing on end. Or maybe it was being here with Callan, the man who had no expectations of her and only a steady admiration in his eyes.

'I know you lost your dad a few years ago, Laurie. So what now? You're an adult. There's no one to disappoint. You can decide what happens next. You can decide what steps you take. Where do you want to go, Laurie? Where do you want to end up?'

The words were measured. His other hand had reached her waist and both were pulling her even closer to him. She could almost hear music in the air between them. And it was as if they weren't talking about her career choice any more. It was so much more than that.

*Where do you want to end up?* The million-dollar question. It was everything that sparked in the air between them. Every impulse that fired in her skin whenever he touched her. Every dream that featured him in high-definition detail.

A smile came across his face. The air in the room was closing in on them. Pressing around every inch. His grip on her waist tightened and he lifted her in the air, as if it were something he did every day, making her breath catch in her throat as he took a few steps and stood her on the thin bench that ran around the inside of the gazebo.

'Maybe it's time to forget, Laurie. Let's pretend you don't need to think about any of these things.' He waited, then reached and wiped another tear from her cheek before adding, 'And neither do I. You told me earlier what you wanted to do. Why don't you just let me give you your dreams tonight?' She heard his voice break and it squeezed at her heart.

Tomorrow everything changed for both of them.

Tomorrow the person who would inherit Annick Castle would be announced. She doubted it would be her. And in a way, she didn't want it to be. She had no idea what to do with a place like Annick Castle, even though it had wound its way into her heart.

Right now, she was more concerned about what it might do to Callan. What it might do to the small boy who had found a haven—a safe place in Annick Castle. It didn't matter what she thought of Angus. It didn't matter to her at all.

All that mattered to her was what Callan

thought of him. How Callan McGregor would feel. Because Callan McGregor was a keeper. She knew that in her heart.

She would never do anything to hurt him. Never do anything to keep him from his dream.

The realisation was startling. Two, in one night.

And even though she couldn't think about it right now they were probably interconnected. The decision about walking away from her job felt freeing. Like spreading her wings and flying high in the air.

She didn't feel guilty about it. She didn't feel irresponsible. It was time to start living her life for herself. Not for anyone else.

Her legs were trembling. She looked around her. It was beautiful. It was the perfect setting. And Callan was the perfect man to share it with.

'Are you going to be my prince tonight, Callan?' She held out her shaking hand towards him.

He gave a little smile. 'Aren't I supposed to be your Rolfe?'

She wrinkled her nose. 'He turned out to be a traitor. I'd rather go with the prince theme.'

He took her hand in his. 'Does this mean I have

to dance and sing? Because, I warn you. This might not work out the way you imagined it.'

Her voice was low and husky. 'You've no idea what I've imagined, Callan.' His eyes widened as his smile spread across his face. He gave a mock bow.

'Ms Jenkins, can I have this dance?'

She gave a little curtsey as he took her hand and her steps quickened around the circular bench. Callan laughed, keeping pace with her as she started to run, letting the rainbow-coloured reflections of light dance across the pale chiffon of her dress. Her gold shoes sparkled in the dim lights but the one thing that stood out for her was the green of Callan's eyes. They didn't leave her. Not for a second.

'You're planning on making me dizzy, aren't you?' he quipped as she started around the circle for the fourth time.

'I might never get to do this again,' came her instant response.

He stopped dead. As if the realisation had just hit him.

Her breath caught in her throat, her heart beating rapidly against her chest. Did she really want this to be the last time for her and Callan?

She could see his quick breaths, see the glimmer of uncertainty across his eyes followed by a look of firm decision.

His hands swept around her waist, lifting her up and spinning her around as if she were as light as a feather. Her arms caught around his neck and she laughed as he continued to spin her round, her dress billowing out around them. He stopped slowly, holding her in place for a few seconds before gradually beginning to lower her down. Her face was just inches above his. She didn't want him to stop touching her; she didn't want him to stop holding her.

'Are you going to kiss me again, Callan?' she whispered. 'Do I get a little warning this time?'

'How much warning do you need?'

'About this much.'

She started to kiss him before he'd completely lowered her to the floor. This time she was ready. This time she initiated it. This time there were no spectators.

There was just her and Callan. A perfect combination.

It wasn't a light kiss. She wasn't gentle. She knew exactly what she was doing. This was happening because she wanted it to happen. This wasn't about her job. This wasn't about Angus McLean. This wasn't about Annick Castle.

This was just about her and Callan.

And it felt so right.

Their kiss was intensifying; the stubble on his chin scraped her skin. His hands ran through her curls, locking into place at the back of her head as he tried to pull her even closer.

The chiffon material on her dress was so thin, all she could feel was the compressed heat from his body against hers.

Her hands ran across the expanse of his back; she could feel his muscles rippling under his shirt. One of these days she'd ask him how he got those.

Or maybe he could show her...

He pulled his head back from hers, still holding her head in place. With slow sensuous movement he slid his hands down her back, around her hips, and stroked upwards with his palms towards her breasts.

She wasn't in a fairy tale any more. She was in a positively adult dream. One where she only dared imagine the outcome.

'Laurie,' he murmured as he rested his forehead against hers.

'Yes.' She could hardly breathe. She would scream if he stopped touching her. This was meant to happen. They were meant to be together.

She'd never felt a connection like this. Her one-track mind knew exactly where this would go. And she couldn't think of a single reason to stop it happening.

She didn't want to have regrets in life. She had too many of those already. And Callan could never be regret. Not when he made her feel like this.

She stood on her tiptoes and kissed his nose. She ran her fingers through his dark hair as she looked into his eyes. He didn't need to ask the question out loud.

She already knew her answer. Her hands

cupped either side of his face. 'Yes, Callan,' she breathed.

And he took her hand in his and led her back to the castle.

# CHAPTER TEN

HE DIDN'T WANT to wake up. He didn't want this day to begin.

This was the day where two things he loved could slip through his fingertips.

All of a sudden he was instantly awake, his eyes fixating on the rain battering on the windowpane. Love. Where had that come from?

With the exception of Angus, Callan couldn't remember the last time he'd ever had a thought like this. Callan 'cared' about people. He didn't love them.

He'd 'cared' about some women in the past. He'd worried about them. He hadn't wanted to hurt their feelings. He'd wanted to take care of them.

None of these things applied to Laurie. He'd have to multiply everything by a thousand to get even close.

From the first second he'd glanced her through the steam on the train platform she'd started to burrow her way under his skin and into his heart.

Her reactions had been totally different from everyone else who could inherit the castle. She'd walked the estate, she'd asked questions, she'd shown an interest that was above and beyond the monetary value. She'd seemed invested in the place.

Her connection with Marion had taken him by surprise. He suspected it had taken Marion by surprise too. She wasn't known for sharing her domain. But apparently Laurie had sneaked under her radar too. She'd done nothing but sing Laurie's praises to him—all with a twinkle in her eyes.

What sat heaviest on his chest was his loyalty to Angus. He knew instantly that if Angus had met Laurie he would have loved her. He would have loved her spark, her inquisitiveness, her cheek and her ability to run rings around Callan.

He just couldn't understand why Angus hadn't met his children. Hadn't loved his children the way he'd loved him. Nothing about it seemed right. And until he could sort that out in his head he would never be able to move forward.

And today was a day for moving forward.

He turned on his side. Laurie currently had her back to him, the cotton sheet had slipped from her shoulders and his eyes carried along the curves of her skin. She was sleeping peacefully and his hands were itching to touch her again.

He wanted to ask her to stay. He wanted to ask her to stay here with him. To stay anywhere with him.

But what could he offer her?

Her words had almost broken his heart last night when she'd told him how she hated her job. It would be so easy for him to tell her just to pack it all in, forget about everything and move up to Edinburgh with him. Money wasn't an object for Callan.

But he knew in his heart that Laurie wasn't that kind of girl.

And the outcome of Annick Castle was still hanging over his head like a black thunder cloud. Until that was resolved his stomach would constantly churn.

He slid his feet to the floor as something flickered into his brain. Laurie had told him she knew who the murderer was. How on earth could she know? He was embarrassed to say that he hadn't been paying enough attention to even hazard a guess.

Was there even a tiny chance that Laurie could inherit the castle?

A shiver crept down his spine. How would that make him feel? He didn't even want to consider that for a second. What was developing between him and Laurie could be destroyed by something like that.

He took a deep breath as he watched her sleeping form. She had a one in twelve chance of inheriting the castle. He watched her gentle breathing, in and out, in and out, her hair framing her face and her tongue running along her rose-pink lips.

He didn't want anything to mess this up. Nothing at all.

He stood up. The boxes. He still hadn't had a chance to go through Angus's boxes. He had to do it now. Time was running out. He might have access to these things now, but in a matter of days he would have to walk away from Annick Castle and leave everything behind. He had to use the opportunity to find out what he could now.

He pulled a shirt over his head and some trousers on. He would do it now while Laurie slept. There was no point disturbing his sleeping Cinderella.

Her eyes flickered open and for a second she was startled. For the last few days she'd woken in a room with a peaceful yellow colour scheme. The pale themes of blue unsettled her. Her reactions were instantaneous. She pulled the sheet over her naked body and flipped over onto her back.

Nothing. No one.

Callan wasn't there.

She was instantly caught by the pain in her chest. The expanse of the bed seemed huge. The dip where he should be lying seemed like a giant chasm. Where was he? Was he embarrassed? Was he ashamed of what had happened last night? Why wasn't he still lying here next to her?

Her beautiful pale pink chiffon dress was lying in a crumpled heap on the floor. Robin would have a fit. Her gold glitter sandals were strewn across the floor, obviously left exactly where they'd fallen. She cringed as she looked around the rest of the room. Even though this was obviously Callan's room, there was no visible sign of him.

It made her stomach churn. She pulled the sheet around her like a toga as she stood up and her eyes swept the room. There was nothing else for her to wear except the clothes she'd discarded last night. And who knew where her underwear was?

She rummaged around the floor eventually finding her bra and pants and pulling them on. Her Liesl dress was a crumpled wreck. It seemed to echo exactly how she felt. Talk about doing the next-day walk of shame.

Thankfully the corridor was empty. She fled down the staircase as quickly as possible and slammed her door closed behind her.

Her half-empty rucksack lay on the floor. Going home. After the announcement today she would be going home.

Her eyes filled with tears. Everything last night with Callan had been perfect. But deep down both of them had known they were saying goodbye.

How could there be a happy ever after for them? What on earth did she expect to happen?

She pulled out some clothes. A pair of Capri pants and a slightly wrinkled shirt that she'd already worn. If she'd thought about it a bit more she could have asked Marion where she could launder her clothes. But there was no point now. No point because she wasn't staying.

There was something pushed under the doorway. She'd completely missed it. She tore the envelope open. Was it from Callan?

Of course it wasn't. He'd left her sleeping alone in his room; why would he push a note under her door? It was from Robin. Asking her to write the name of the person she suspected as the murderer and return it to him before eleven that morning.

That was easy. She grabbed a pen and scribbled the name. She didn't even have to think about it.

Part of her wanted to hide away in her room. *Her* room. It wasn't her room. It was part of the castle. After today she would probably never see this place again and it was about time she accepted that.

She'd probably never see Callan again. But that thought made her legs buckle and left her sitting on the window seat looking out at the crashing sea.

The rain was battering down outside. It was the first day of bad weather she'd experienced here and all of a sudden she felt very sorry for the bygone smugglers. It must be terrifying down at the caves in weather like this. She could feel the wind whistle through the panes of glass. The temperature was distinctly lower. Or maybe it was just her mood.

It was time to step away from Annick Castle and Callan McGregor. It was time to go back to London and sort her life out.

One thing hadn't changed. She didn't want to be a lawyer any more and she needed to take steps to make a change. She could do that. She could do that now.

Annick Castle had changed her. It had given her some perspective on life. Meeting some of her unknown relatives had been enlightening.

She would have preferred it if some of them had remained unknown. But there was a few she had felt some kind of affinity towards. She would love to go and visit her auntie Mary in Ireland some time. She would love to show her some more pictures of her father so she could see the family resemblance between the two of them.

As for Angus McLean? She'd grown tired of wondering why he'd abandoned his children. She'd grown tired of wondering why he'd been able to show love to some unknown child, then split his heart in two with the contents of his will.

She'd grown tired of it all.

There was a thin layer of dust over the boxes. No one had touched them in years.

He'd found them in the back of a cupboard in Angus's room, hidden amongst shoes and old smoking jackets. He'd been curious at first, wondering if they would reveal something about Angus's unacknowledged children.

But they were something else entirely.

Medical files. And lots of them.

It took Callan a few minutes to work out what

he was looking at. At first they seemed totally random. Patients allocated numbers instead of names. They were ancient—some more than seventy years old. And the initial sense of unease he'd felt at looking at someone's medical files rapidly diminished.

The files all seemed to have one thing in common. A big red stamp with deceased across the front.

But there was more than that. All of these people seemed to have died within a very short period of time. A window of six months back in the 1940s just after the Second World War had ended.

It took him a little longer to work out entirely what they were telling him.

Angus's father had owned a pharmaceutical company. These were all records of drug trials. Nowadays clinical drug trials were scrutinised, monitored and regulated beyond all recognition. Seventy-five years ago—not so much.

And whatever drug these people had been trialling seemed to have had an extreme adverse effect. All the patients taking it had died within six months.

All except one. Patient X115. Otherwise known as Angus McLean.

It was a horrible moment of realisation. Scribbled notes were all over the file that was obviously Angus's.

Scribbled notes that revealed that as one drug trial patient after another died, Angus McLean had fully expected to die himself within a few months.

He'd had no idea what was wrong with the medication, but all the other patients—twenty of them—had died within a short space of time.

Callan leaned back against the desk. He'd been sitting on the floor, the files scattered all around him. People had been paid a fee all those years ago to take part in drug trials. Things weren't so carefully monitored. And although the medical files were full of things he didn't understand, there were a few things that he did understand.

According to the post-mortem results most of the patients had died of some kind of accelerated blood disorder. Angus McLean had thought he was living on borrowed time. He'd fully expected to die along with the rest of the group.

Except he hadn't. He'd outlived them all by almost seventy years.

Was this the reason? The reason why he hadn't had contact with his children, but had instead made some kind of financial recompense?

From the dates he could see, at least three of his children had been born during wartime. Communications were limited. It wasn't like today where a ping of an email signified the arrival of a message from halfway round the globe. He'd moved around a lot during, and directly after, the war. It was entirely possible that Angus hadn't found out about some of his children until after the war—right around the time he'd just taken part in the disastrous drug trial.

Callan's head was spinning. He couldn't really draw any conclusions from this. He was guessing.

But Angus had been a gentle-natured man. Callan didn't really want to believe he'd deliberately left his children without a father. But how would Angus have coped, forming a relationship with these children, whilst he was living in fear he would die at any moment? Leave them to suffer the bereavement of losing their dad? Maybe, if Angus had died quickly, it would have been better not to meet them. And although he didn't agree with it, he could maybe understand it a little better.

But Angus would never have left his children unsupported. That did seem like something he would do. Provide for them. And if this was the only explanation Callan could find, then he'd take it.

Maybe he'd thought leaving them Annick Castle would make up for the fact they hadn't had a father figure in their lives. How had he felt as one year after another had passed? Had he realised he'd managed to run the gauntlet that the others in the drug trial had failed?

Callan leaned forward. There was a collection of black-and-white photos at the bottom of the box. Some of women. Some of children. One, a picture of Angus with his arm around a woman.

This was it. This was the only sign that Angus

McLean actually had family. No letters. No gushy cards. No sentimental keepsakes.

Callan felt a rush of unease at the similarities between himself and Angus.

If someone searched his personal belongings what would they find? No pictures or memorabilia about his father. No trace of the man at all. One slightly crumpled picture of his mother, along with an album of family snaps of him as a baby or a young boy accompanied by an unknown arm holding him, or a set of unidentified legs.

He opened the lid of the other box, fully expecting to find similar contents. But this was different. This held a leather-bound photo album.

He opened the first page. It was some old pictures of Angus as a young boy with his mother and father. Family snaps had obviously been few and far between then.

He flipped the pages. Angus as he was growing up. In school uniform. In hunting gear. In his army uniform. In a dinner suit.

And then there was Callan. As a small child sitting at the kitchen table that still existed, laughing heartily with Angus laughing next to him. Callan had no recollection of the picture ever being taken, but that tiny snapshot in time struck him like a bullet through his heart.

He flicked again. Him and Angus on every page. Fishing. Horse-riding. Sitting in the grounds. Digging the gardens with Bert. Standing on the cannons in the castle grounds. Sailing across the swan pond in the most rickety paddle boat that ever existed. It had subsequently sunk to the bottom of the pond never to be seen again.

Callan standing at the castle doors holding some kind of certificate in his hands. He had a vague recollection of it being his exam results that gained him his place at university. All little moments in time.

He'd been feeling annoyed. He'd been feeling spurned by the fact Angus wouldn't sell him Annick Castle. Deep down he'd been hurt that Angus hadn't considered him in his will.

But here it was. Captured for posterity. Exactly what Angus had left him.

A life.

A safe haven.

Love.

The things he'd needed to shape him and become his own man.

A tear dripped down his face.

Now he understood.

He'd always known how much he'd owed Angus. But here was something to cherish and keep. To help him remember that memories were more precious than material things. None of Angus's children had shared any of these moments with him.

The gift that Angus had left him was the most precious of all.

# CHAPTER ELEVEN

THE GONG SOUNDED dead on eleven. Laurie had never heard the gong used before. She'd noticed it standing in the entrance hall and wondered what it had ever been used for. It was almost like the start of one of those movies, except Robin wasn't dressed in a loincloth.

Everyone was gathering in the drawing room. It seemed to be the room where Angus's relatives had spent most of their time.

The rain was battering the windows with a ferocity she'd never seen. It seemed fitting on a day like this. It was almost as if the weather could read how she was feeling.

She filed in and took a seat. Frank, the family lawyer, was standing in the corner of the room. He looked as if he wanted to be sick. Robin stood next to him along with the guy John who had been playing the butler, and the girl who'd been murdered on Friday night.

There was the sound of hurried footsteps outside. Callan appeared with Marion and Bert by his side. It was only fitting. They should all hear who would own Annick Castle together.

Her eyes fixed on the floor. After Callan had abandoned her in the bedroom she didn't even want to look him in the eye. She certainly didn't want to have a conversation with him in front of anyone else. Whatever she had to say to Callan she could say in private before she left.

But Callan seemed to have entirely different thoughts.

He crossed the room in a matter of seconds, sitting on the chaise longue next to her. 'Laurie, I'm sorry. I had to go and look through Angus's papers this morning. You won't believe what I've found.'

*What?* Her head whipped up. She couldn't help but frown. 'But you left this morning.' She shook her head. 'I woke up and you were gone.' She couldn't hide the confusion in her voice. And she didn't care what he'd found.

He smiled, obviously unaware of the turmoil she'd felt. 'You looked so peaceful. I didn't want to wake you. I meant to come back and bring you breakfast in bed, but once I started going through Angus's boxes I just lost all track of time.'

There was no time to reply. No time to try and think clearly. Frank cleared his throat loudly. 'Thank you for gathering here this morning. In accordance with Angus McLean's will, today we will reveal who has inherited Annick Castle. Once the announcement is made, we will make suitable arrangements for a DNA test to be carried out to confirm the family connection. Once this has been confirmed, the process of passing on Annick Castle will take a few weeks.'

Frank looked around the room. He was clutching cards in his hands—the cards where everyone had written who they thought had carried out the murder.

He was obviously feeling the strain. The colour in his face was rising, probably in line with his blood pressure. He gave a nervous smile. 'It turns out that only one person correctly identified the murderer. There was provision in the will if more than one person had guessed correctly, but that won't be necessary now.'

Heads were glancing around the room. Everyone wondering who had been right. 'So, who was the murderer?' Craig snapped, the tension obviously getting too much for him.

Frank nodded. 'The murderer was John. The butler did it,' he said simply.

There were gasps around the room, along with several expletives.

'That's not fair!'

'I hardly spoke to him.'

'He was only ever in the background.'

'I never even had a conversation with him!'

Robin was instantly on the defensive. 'We conducted everything with absolute precision. The clues were all there if you looked for them.'

Laurie was frozen. Her throat dried in an instant. She couldn't hear anything. She couldn't hear because the thudding in her ears was getting louder and louder. Sweat. She'd never experienced sweat like it. Appearing instantly all over her body, running down the length of her back and collecting between the cups of her bra. She was freezing. She felt as if someone had just plucked up her body and dropped her in the raging sea outside.

People were still ranting. Callan was just frozen in the chair beside her, holding his breath while he waited for the announcement.

The announcement that would mean any chance they had of having any kind of relationship would disappear in an instant.

Frank's grey eyes locked on hers. 'Congratulations, Laurie. Pending a DNA test, Annick Castle is yours.'

The room erupted.

'It's a fix!'

'She's obviously in league with Frank—you lawyers stick together.'

'She's hardly even been here!'

'She's in cahoots with that man—Callan. The rest of us never really stood a chance!'

She felt numb. There was good reason she didn't like some of her relatives. Her vibes about most of them hadn't been wrong. Any tiny flicker of doubts she'd had about the personality traits of some her relatives were now being revealed in 3D multicolour. She felt as if she couldn't breathe.

The air was coming in, but she couldn't get it back out.

From the corner of her eye she saw her auntie Mary give her a little smile and blow her a kiss. She was sitting on the other side of the room and her elderly bones couldn't possibly navigate the melee between them.

It was the first sign of hope. The first glimmer of a good-luck wish.

She was scared to look sideways. She was scared to look at Callan. Part of her wished he'd jumped up to defend her once the rabble had started. But he hadn't—he'd been silent.

Frank was trying to push his way through the crowd. At this point it looked as if he might be trampled by the objectors.

She stood up and turned to face Callan.

He hadn't moved. He looked shell-shocked. The smile on his face earlier had vanished. His green eyes lifted and met hers.

She could read everything on his face and in his eyes. He'd been taking steps forward. He'd been trying to move past the fact that Annick

Castle would be inherited by someone else. And he'd been getting there. In tiny baby steps.

But this was entirely different. This changed everything. The pain and confusion was etched in his eyes. Both of them knew this wasn't her fault. This was something that neither of them had control over. Or did they?

Could she have done something to prevent this happening? Could she have done something to allow them to cling onto the hope of developing a relationship together?

She was so confused right now.

Panic started to grip her. She'd written that name on the card without a second thought. Her reactions had been automatic. She should have guessed wrongly. But it hadn't even occurred to her at the time.

Pain started to spread across her chest. She was starting to feel woozy. The room was closing in around her. She couldn't bear the look on Callan's face. The look that said everything had just changed. His pain was too much for her to bear. And the ramifications made her feel as if everything was out of her control.

Her feet started to move. She started to push her way through the bodies. She had to get outside. She had to get some air.

Marion reached out to her on the way past but she didn't even slow her steps. She couldn't.

She pulled the main door open. The wind and rain howled around her but she didn't even care. She just walked. And kept on walking.

Her shirt was soaked in seconds, her hair whipping around her face. But all she could think about was the air. It was what she needed.

Her legs carried her around to the front of the castle—the most exposed edge facing the sea. She leaned against the wall and tried to take some deep breaths.

The wind was working against her—almost sucking the air from her lungs as she tried to pull it in. She bent over, arms around her waist and counted to ten. One, two, three…

She lifted her head again. This time she felt the cold coursing through her. This time she looked at the castle she could inherit.

Tears started to pour down her cheeks. This was hers. This *could* be hers.

It was almost unbelievable. To go from a girl with only one known living relative, to a girl with a huge array of aunts, uncles and cousins, and the inheritor of a castle all in the space of a few weeks.

The castle loomed in front of her. Dominant. Intimidating. A whole world of problems.

But she didn't feel like that about it. She looked at the sandy-coloured storm-battered building with its intricate-paned glass windows and drum towers.

She loved it.

She loved it with her whole heart.

But she loved something or someone else a whole lot more.

Genetically she might have a right to Annick Castle. But there were some things so much more important than genes.

'Laurie!' The shout came from her side.

Callan was running towards her, followed by Frank bundled up in a rainproof mac. Frank's umbrella caught in the high winds, turning instantly inside out and making him spin around blindly.

Callan reached her, soaked and windswept by the battering rain. He put his hands on either side of her shoulders. 'Laurie, are you okay? What happened? You ran out before we had a chance to talk.'

She shook her head. Would he notice her tears in amongst the torrent of rain?

Callan was shaking his head in wonder. An amazed smile appeared on his face. 'How did you know? How did you know it was the butler? We've hardly been there this weekend.' He was shouting now. She could hardly hear him above the roar of the waves below.

She lifted her hands. 'Who else could it be? There were twelve of us. It couldn't be any of us, Callan. That would have been unfair. It had to be you, Robin or John. And when the murder took place, you had your arm around me the whole time.'

The recognition dawned on his face. He'd obviously never given the whole weekend much thought. He'd been too wrapped up in the outcome. Too wrapped up in the fate of Annick Castle.

He grabbed her hand. Frank had reached him now and was starting to babble. She couldn't hear a single word he was saying in the braying winds. 'Come on,' shouted Callan. 'Let's get inside.'

He pulled her towards a back door. It must have been a servants' entrance and it took them along a back corridor until they reached somewhere she was much more familiar with. Much more comfortable with—the library.

Callan waited until Frank had joined them and locked the door behind them. Rain was dripping from every part of her. Callan lifted a throw from the back of one of the chairs and stood in front of her, gently rubbing her sodden hair and face.

Callan was so wrapped up in what he wanted to tell her he couldn't contain himself. 'I found medical files, Laurie. Files that were part of a drug trial seventy years ago. Angus was a participant. Everyone else died within six months. He must have thought he was going to die too, Laurie. That's why he didn't meet his kids—just provided for them financially.'

She hadn't spoken. She hadn't responded. And his voice tailed off to be replaced with a concerned expression on his face. There was a second of recognition. Recognition that she was long past the point of caring about Angus McLean.

'Laurie? Isn't this what you wanted? You're the only relative here who has shown any real interest in Annick Castle.' He hesitated. 'I'll need to go over the castle accounts with you, but some of the things you suggested might be part of the way forward for Annick Castle.'

Frank stepped forward. 'I have to warn you I think there might be some legal challenges from some of the unhappy parties. There's nothing we can do to prevent that. But no matter what their challenges, Angus's will is rock solid. He made sure of that. It might just tie us up in court proceedings for some time.' He rustled some papers. 'Now, can we make some arrangements for your DNA test? It's just a simple cheek swab, and I'd expect the results back relatively quickly.'

'Stop.' She lifted her hand. 'Stop it. Both of you.'

Callan froze. He'd been mid-rub of her hair, which was still stubbornly dripping on the floor below. She shivered. The impact of the rain and wind was starting to affect her body's reactions. Frank's mouth was still open—poised mid-sentence.

'I can't do this.'

'What?' Both voices, in perfect unison.

Callan's brow instantly wrinkled. 'What do you mean you can't do this? You are the perfect person to do this, Laurie.'

'No. No, I'm not.' She shook her head fiercely. 'If I'd thought about this more carefully I would have put the wrong name on the card.' Frank looked horrified, but she continued before he could say anything else. 'I'm not the right person to look after Annick Castle. It doesn't matter that I'm a relative of Angus McLean. It doesn't matter at all.'

She walked over and picked up one of the photographs of Angus in his army uniform. 'I didn't know this man. I didn't know this man at all.' She pointed to herself. 'And he didn't know me. I didn't matter to him. My father didn't matter to him. I don't care what his reasons were.'

Her brain felt as if it were scrambled. She didn't feel rational. She didn't feel in control.

'Laurie, hold on. Let me show you what I found—'

'No. Don't, Callan. I don't want to hear it. The fact is, I'm a lawyer. And I'm not even going to be that for much longer. But it doesn't matter. What do I know about a place like this? I wouldn't even know where to begin. It's already starting to fall apart.' She held out her hands. 'This is a piece of history. This is something that should be protected and preserved. This is something that other people should enjoy.'

'But you can do that, Laurie. You've already considered what could happen with Annick Castle. Let me tell you what I found.'

She felt herself start to sway. Her legs were turning to jelly underneath her and she slumped down into one of the nearby chairs.

She took a few seconds, then lifted her head. 'Frank, if you need to do a DNA test on me, then that's fine. Do it. But I need you to do something else for me.'

'What?' Frank looked bewildered, as if the

whole event were taking place in a parallel universe.

She loved Callan. She absolutely loved him. If she kept Annick Castle they would never have a chance. This would always be Callan's home. And she would always be the person that had taken that away from him. And she loved him too much for that.

She'd seen the flash in his eyes back in the drawing room. She didn't need him to spell it all out to her.

She wanted to believe that he really hadn't meant to leave her this morning. But deep down she couldn't entirely be *sure*.

And she needed to be sure. She needed to know that Callan McGregor was with her because he wanted to be, not because she was a route to something else that he loved.

She needed him to love her, just as much as she loved him. The only way to find out if that was true was to take Annick Castle out of the equation.

To put right something that was wrong.

She looked over at Callan's face. She loved him.

She loved him with her whole heart. There was only one action she could take right now and it was something she was proud to say that her dad had taught her. *Do the right thing.*

'I want to give Annick Castle to Callan. I want the castle to be looked after by the person who deserves it most.'

# CHAPTER TWELVE

'WHAT?'

Callan couldn't believe his ears. This day was getting madder by the second.

'You can't do that.'

'Yes, I think you'll find I can. Can't I, Frank?'

Frank nodded numbly.

Callan knelt down in front of Laurie. She looked exhausted and she was still soaking wet. They were all soaking wet. 'Laurie, you've had a shock. You're not thinking clearly.'

Her words were crisp. 'I'm thinking perfectly clearly, Callan. If Annick Castle is mine, then I can do what I want with it.'

He shook his head. 'But Angus wanted it to go to family. *You're* his family, Laurie, not me.'

She leaned forward, her face inches away from his. 'And I can see exactly how much that hurts you, Callan. What is a family anyway? Is it the person that created you genetically? Or is it the person that's loved you, protected you and sheltered you from the world? Isn't family the people who've taken care of you, helped you do your homework, played with you and looked out for you when you were a kid? Shaped you into the adult you've become? What does the word family mean to you, Callan?' She reached out her finger and touched his chest. 'What does it mean to you in here?'

He couldn't speak. He felt totally blindsided by her. It was as if she could see inside his head. See every bad thought that had entered his brain. Every time he'd bitten his tongue this weekend to stop him saying something he shouldn't.

He knew exactly what she meant. He'd heard her talk about her father. She'd loved him unconditionally—much like the way he'd loved Angus. Whenever she was thinking deeply about something she fingered the gold locket around her neck, the one her father had given her. The love she felt for her father had lasted long after her father's death. And he felt the same; he'd never forget Angus.

'Angus was my family,' he whispered. His throat felt dry and scratchy. Saying the words still hurt. Facing up to the fact that Angus hadn't thought of him as family still hurt. But now he'd discovered so much more.

He reached over and took her hand. 'Let me show you something—something I just found.'

He didn't wait for her response; he just pulled her along behind him. Down the corridor and up the carved staircase towards the room that held Angus's things.

Laurie hadn't stopped crying yet. Slow tears were still trickling down her cheeks. She reached over and put her hand on his cheek. 'What is it, Callan? Because I can't deal with this right now. I can't deal with you.' She pressed her hand to her chest.

He dropped down onto the carpet and pulled the photo album from the top of the box. 'I don't want you to give me the castle, Laurie. It's not right. It's not the way it's supposed to be.'

She lifted her head up. He could see the determined look across her face. The kind of look that dared anyone to argue with her. 'I don't agree with what Angus has done. And I don't need to. But I can put right what I think is wrong.'

Callan shook his head. Every other relative had looked as if they wanted to sell the castle. Laurie was the only person who hadn't considered that. Did she have any idea what the castle was really worth?

'Laurie, I have to tell you. I'd planned to speak to whoever inherited the castle to see if they would accept my offer. I'd always planned to try and buy Annick Castle. I certainly don't want you to give it to me.' He placed the album in her hands. 'But this is what Angus McLean left me. Something so much more important than a castle.'

He was starting to panic. This didn't feel right. Callan McGregor was always entirely above board. He didn't want Laurie to give him the castle. No way.

How would that look?

Particularly now—when he wanted her to stay.

This confused everything. He'd wanted to ask her to stay this morning. Before any of this happened. And he should have asked her. He should have asked her then.

He wanted her to understand everything. He wanted her to look through the album and realise he believed she was right. The gift that Angus had given him was security. A place where a little boy could thrive and be loved by a family. The people who stayed here were his family. Blood didn't matter. Genetics didn't matter.

But Laurie's face was blank. Was she listening to him at all? She still hadn't opened the album. The album that told the story of his life. He had to try something else.

'I'll buy it from you. We'll get an independent survey, an independent evaluation.' He was starting to babble, but he just couldn't help it. He felt as if everything was slipping through his fingers. Which was strange, because up until a few days ago his priority had been Annick Castle. A few days ago, this would have been exactly what he wanted.

And part of him still wanted it. Just not without her.

He shook his head. 'I've looked at the accounts.

Things aren't good. Annick Castle is in trouble. The nest egg that Angus used to have just isn't there any more. You've seen for yourself that there are areas that need attention. And with a place like this there are no simple fixes. Even things that seem simple need a master craftsman. Traditional materials, specialist trades, everything has to meet the standards for listed building consent. Things need to change around here.'

Laurie stood up. 'What are you talking about, Callan? I've told you. I want to give you Annick Castle. I don't want your money. I don't want you to buy it from me. It doesn't even feel as if it should really be mine.' She flung her hands in the air, letting the album fall to the floor. 'It's ridiculous. I inherit this place on the basis of the name I wrote on a card?' She turned to face Frank too. 'Tell me this isn't fundamentally wrong—because we all know it is. This place, never mind its monetary value, what about its heritage value, its history? These are the things that are important. These are the things that make Annick Castle special.' She turned back to Callan. 'Angus was wrong. Annick Castle should always have been yours. You're the one with the connection with this place. You're the one who loves it. It should be yours.' There was real passion in her voice. As if she knew, as if she understood.

And he could recognise it. Because he understood completely.

He placed his hand on her arm. 'But that's just it, Laurie. I'm not the only one with a connection to this place, am I?'

He watched her eyes widen. She started to stutter, 'B-but…'

'Tell me.' He stepped forward and placed his hand on her chest. 'Tell me how Annick Castle makes you feel in here, Laurie.'

She didn't answer. She couldn't answer.

'I could see it, Laurie. I could see it in your eyes, in everything you did this weekend. From the moment you saw this place, from the moment you set foot in this place, Annick Castle started to get under your skin. You asked questions, you took an interest in everything that happens around here. You looked at this place with a fresh set of eyes.' His voice lowered. 'You introduced me to ideas that I would never have considered myself.' He shook his head as he grew more determined—as he started to see in his head exactly what he wanted to happen.

It was like standing at the railway station again, watching the smoke clear around Laurie's curves. He just knew.

'I can't do this without you, Laurie. I don't want to do this without you. This morning, when I woke up I watched you sleeping. I wanted to ask you then. I should have asked you then.'

'Asked me what?'

'To stay. To stay with me.' The words that had been skirting around the edges of his brain for the last few hours. It was so much easier to say them out loud than he could possibly have imagined.

He sat her down on the chaise longue next to the window and put the album in her lap, flicking past the first few pages of Angus's photographs and onto the pages that showed him as a young boy.

He could see her sharp intake of breath. 'Laurie, I don't care what you do with Annick Castle. If I ever want to move on, I have to let it go. I have to get past this. But I can't get past you.'

Her eyes widened as he turned the pages, letting her see every year of his life recorded by Angus. Letting her see the love between them, letting her see the warmth and security that he'd been provided with. Letting her see his family.

'What is this?' she murmured.

'This is me. This is the legacy that Angus left me.' He put his hand over hers and squeezed tightly. 'It means so much more than bricks and mortar. Angus, and the people here, helped me grow into the man I am today.' He traced a finger down her cheek. 'One that knows if you love someone, you should always put them first.'

Her voice trembled. 'What do you mean you can't get past me, Callan? What are you saying?'

'I'm saying whatever your decision—about Annick Castle, or about your job—I want to be in your life. I want to be part of your life.' He put both of his hands on her cheeks. 'I want to be your family.'

Tears glistened in her eyes.

'You have to know that I've never connected with anyone the way I've connected with you. I don't want to let you go. I don't want this weekend to end.' He held up his arms. 'I wanted to ask you to stay with me this morning, Laurie, but I didn't know where I'd be. I didn't know what I'd have to offer you.'

Her voice cracked. 'Why would you need to offer me anything, Callan? I don't expect anything from you.'

'But that's just it, Laurie. I want you to. I want to be part of your life. I want to be here for you. Wherever you want to be, just tell me. I can find a way to make this work.'

He could see her breath catching in her throat.

Her head was spinning. He was asking her to stay. He was telling her he wanted to be with her. But he hadn't said the words. The three little words she needed to hear.

She took his hands from her cheeks and intertwined her fingers with his. It had finally stopped raining and the sun was peeking out from behind some clouds. Beneath them the gardens lay out in all their coloured glory. Who wouldn't want to look out at that every single day?

She took a deep breath. 'I've been so confused, Callan. You're right. From the moment I set foot in Annick Castle I feel as if it's got a hold on me. I love this place. I love every single part of it.'

She hesitated. Should she say the next part?

'You've made some of my dreams come true, Callan. I never expected it. I never imagined it.'

His hand clasped over hers. 'Every girl should have their own *Sound of Music* gazebo. Every girl should have their own princess staircase.'

'But I don't want every girl to have you.' Did she just say that out loud? In another life she might have cringed, but not here, and not now. This was the moment she found out if her life was going to change for ever.

His voice was low and sincere. 'Every girl can't have me. There's only one girl I want. There's only one girl I want in my life, now and always.' His hand reached up and stroked her cheek. 'Know that I will go anywhere with you, any time.' He shrugged his shoulders. 'I can Blether all over the world, but there's no one else I want to blether with. It's you or nobody. I love you, Laurie Jenkins. Please say you'll stay with me. Please say we have a future together.'

She reached up and caught his finger in her

hand. 'I love you too. I can't imagine spending a single day without you.'

She was going to cry again. The tears were building in her eyes.

'Can I interest you in an Edinburgh town house, Laurie Jenkins?'

'Can I interest you in a slightly dishevelled castle, Callan McGregor?'

He smiled, his eyes crinkling as pulled her towards him in a kiss. 'Let's begin negotiations. I think I'm going to need a good lawyer.'

She laughed. 'I know just the person.'

## EPILOGUE

As soon as he walked through the doors all he could smell was the wonderful array of baking. Gingerbread, chocolate cake, freshly baked scones and the bubbling smell of lentil soup. His stomach growled in instant response but there was a bus tour due in an hour. He had to keep his mind on the job. 'Laurie, where are you?'

The former icehouse was exactly as she'd planned. Windows all the way around showing views of the gardens and views of the sea. Red and white checked tablecloths, comfortable chairs at the tables, a separate play area for kids and a *very* expensive coffee machine that Callan had already burned himself on. Still, it was red and matched perfectly. *And* it had put a huge smile on Laurie's face.

She appeared from behind the counter, looking a little flushed, wiping her hands on a towel. 'It can't be that time already?'

He raised his eyebrows. 'It is.'

'But I haven't got changed, or fixed my hair, and my make-up must be halfway down my face.'

He shook his head and put his hands on her waist. 'You look perfect.'

'But I've still to—'

He bent down and kissed her to stop her talking. It was amazing how often he had to do that. But it worked like a charm every time. She wound her hands around his neck. 'You're distracting me,' she murmured.

'It's my job.'

He pulled back and smiled. 'I have two special customers that we can't keep waiting.'

Fourteen months of blood, sweat, tears and lots and lots of special memories. Annick Castle was theirs. Together. And it was now open to the public. The repairs had been put in order. They'd been exhausting and daunting. There had been hours of planning and negotiations with local authorities. They'd even had to redo the steps down the cliff side and install a proper handrail.

But the important thing was that they'd done them together.

And the truth was he'd never seen her look happier. She gave a nervous laugh. 'Customers. Now I'm really scared.'

'Oh, don't worry. I think they'll like this place,' he said with confidence as she flicked the sign on the door from Closed to Open.

Marion and Bert didn't waste any time. Bert went straight to the strawberry and cream sponge sitting under a glass dome. 'I'll have a bit of that and a mug of tea.' He wagged his finger at Laurie. 'Don't be giving me any of those fancy china cups.'

Marion was the extreme opposite. 'I'll have a toasted scone with butter and jam, and a pot of tea.' She nodded at Laurie. 'And I do want a china cup.'

Laurie scurried off, obviously overjoyed by her first customers. Callan sat down at one of the round tables, staring out at the crashing ocean. It was August. The doors to Annick Castle opened today. His stomach was churning a little at the thought of it.

Part of it was genuine nerves about what people might think of the place he loved. Part of it was fear that things wouldn't work out. Laurie would be devastated. He was beginning to suspect she loved this place even more than he did. Could that even be possible?

He heard the clink of china being set on a table, appreciative voices, then he felt a hand on his back and Laurie slid into the chair next to him, putting a large piece of his favourite chocolate cake on the table in front of him.

'How does it feel?'

She smiled and glanced out of the window, looking the other way towards the gardens. 'It feels right,' she said quietly as she reached over and squeezed his hands.

'No regrets about leaving London?'

She shook her head fiercely. 'Not a single one. I haven't had a tension headache since I moved here.'

'Even with all the hassles with the castle?'

'They weren't hassles. They were teething problems.' She leaned over and kissed him. 'Besides I had someone I could moan to every night in bed with me.'

He gave her a wink as he put a piece of chocolate cake in his mouth. 'I hope that wasn't the only reason you were moaning.' He didn't wait for her reaction before he let out a yelp. 'Ouch! What's that?'

Laurie jumped up. 'What's wrong? Is there something wrong with the cake?'

'There's something very wrong. I just got a lump of something in it.' He couldn't stop the gleam in his eyes as he pretended to fish something out of his mouth.

She still hadn't clicked. 'What is it?' she demanded as she made a grab for his palm. 'Oh!'

The emerald and diamond ring lay in the palm of his hand. He'd wanted to propose to her from the moment she'd moved here. But there was never a more perfect time than now—the first day of their new life together.

'Is that all you can say—oh?'

She smiled. 'Oh, no, you don't, Callan McGregor. I want the whole shebang.'

He slid down onto the floor, kneeling in front

of her. 'I should have taken you to the gazebo, shouldn't I?'

She leaned forward and whispered in his ear. 'Don't worry, our last trip to the gazebo seems to have left us with more than memories.'

'Really?' He jumped straight back up and pulled her into his arms, swinging her around. 'Really?' He couldn't believe it. Nothing could be more perfect.

'Really.' She smiled as he lowered her to the floor.

For the first time in years Callan felt flustered. He grabbed the ring and knelt down again in front of her. 'Then I better make this quick, before people start getting out calendars and looking at the date.' He took both her hands in his. 'Laurie Jenkins, I love you more than life itself. Will you do me the honour of walking down our gorgeous staircase in a wedding dress and becoming my wife?' He slid the ring onto her finger.

'I think you're supposed to wait for my answer.' She smiled.

He leaned forward and kissed her, laying his

hand gently on her stomach. 'It seems to me that you've already realised I've got no patience. How about we get ready for a castle full of them?'

'I can't wait,' she replied as she kissed him again and again.

* * * * *

# Mills & Boon® Large Print
## September 2014

**THE ONLY WOMAN TO DEFY HIM**
Carol Marinelli

**SECRETS OF A RUTHLESS TYCOON**
Cathy Williams

**GAMBLING WITH THE CROWN**
Lynn Raye Harris

**THE FORBIDDEN TOUCH OF SANGUARDO**
Julia James

**ONE NIGHT TO RISK IT ALL**
Maisey Yates

**A CLASH WITH CANNAVARO**
Elizabeth Power

**THE TRUTH ABOUT DE CAMPO**
Jennifer Hayward

**EXPECTING THE PRINCE'S BABY**
Rebecca Winters

**THE MILLIONAIRE'S HOMECOMING**
Cara Colter

**THE HEIR OF THE CASTLE**
Scarlet Wilson

**TWELVE HOURS OF TEMPTATION**
Shoma Narayanan

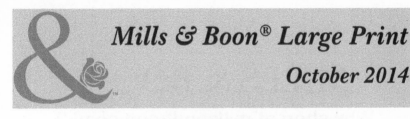

## *Mills & Boon® Large Print*
### *October 2014*

**RAVELLI'S DEFIANT BRIDE**
Lynne Graham

**WHEN DA SILVA BREAKS THE RULES**
Abby Green

**THE HEARTBREAKER PRINCE**
Kim Lawrence

**THE MAN SHE CAN'T FORGET**
Maggie Cox

**A QUESTION OF HONOUR**
Kate Walker

**WHAT THE GREEK CAN'T RESIST**
Maya Blake

**AN HEIR TO BIND THEM**
Dani Collins

**BECOMING THE PRINCE'S WIFE**
Rebecca Winters

**NINE MONTHS TO CHANGE HIS LIFE**
Marion Lennox

**TAMING HER ITALIAN BOSS**
Fiona Harper

**SUMMER WITH THE MILLIONAIRE**
Jessica Gilmore

# MILLS & BOON®

## Why shop at millsandboon.co.uk?

Each year, thousands of romance readers find their perfect read at millsandboon.co.uk. That's because we're passionate about bringing you the very best romantic fiction. Here are some of the advantages of shopping at www.millsandboon.co.uk:

* **Get new books first**—you'll be able to buy your favourite books one month before they hit the shops

* **Get exclusive discounts**—you'll also be able to buy our specially created monthly collections, with up to 50% off the RRP

* **Find your favourite authors**—latest news, interviews and new releases for all your favourite authors and series on our website, plus ideas for what to try next

* **Join in**—once you've bought your favourite books, don't forget to register with us to rate, review and join in the discussions

Visit **www.millsandboon.co.uk**
for all this and more today!